I0596403

"Wonderful & Terrifying Nightmares"
By Stephen W. Scott

All of the people, places, organizations, and events portrayed in these stories are either works of fiction or are used fictitiously.

ISBN 979-8298881494

Copyright © 2025

Book cover design by Derek Stewart

FOREWARD

Nightmares are wonderful for horror writers. Where else can we get good ideas? Also, I love oxymorons! How else can you get "Wonderful & Terrible Nightmares." I never dreamed I could make money off scaring people with the stuff that scares me.

I try to write a scary short story around Halloween, and most of these tales were created during that time of the year. I love Halloween. Who doesn't like trick-or-treating, eating candy, scary movies, stories, of the things that go "bump" in the night?

Wonderful & Terrifying Nightmares is my opus to the Twilight Zone, Dark Shadows, and Tales from the Crypt episodes that kept me up at night. I wish I could get away with small intros and outros – and I can hear them recited by Rod Serling.

Fear is the one emotion that triggers the worst of our imagination. Like HP Lovecraft noted, it is the oldest and most common fears. Those things that frighten us, real and imagined, often run our lives. Usually, we run from the past and balk when approaching the future. We fear what we do not understand whether it is rejection from a significant other (parent, spouse, sibling, child, peer), or a death, a monster, fire, injury, or some sort of supernatural entity. As we get older, that fear becomes more prescient, although as adults, we are more prepared for that venture. Fear is where we find the Twilight Zone and Dark Shadows episodes in our lives.

"Night of the Crows" is one of my favorites, and the second story I ever got published. I was very happy create a nod to "The Wizard of Oz," and use a scarecrow to provide the menacing fear to a young boy. It was published in the early 2000s from a paying website, horrorfind.com (not out there anymore).

"Pumpkin Light" is an unpublished short story I wrote in the early 2000s is another one that deals with the death of parents, as well as untapped anger in the midst of loss. I dedicate this one to my Uncle Don.

"Tongues Afire" is another one in the mid-2000s. I got the inspiration for this while teaching at a small rural school. After lunch, students would go outside to play games, run around, and be kids. One day, some junior high girls ganged up to ostracize and bully another girl who was new to the school. A colleague of mine dealt with the situation as I watched the new girl reduced to utter tears.

"Angry Highway" was written during an angry part of

my life while I lived in Texas. Feeling as if I took a wrong turn, I used my isolation and anger, along with my Driver's Education background, to craft a tale of road rage everyone seems to feel when on the angry and lonely roads of life.

"Blind Nightmares" was written in the mid-2000s and is the precursor for *"Do You Hear What I Hear?"* I finally got it published in the anthology, **"Flash of the Dead: Halloween 2024"** last year.

The darkest story, *"Slish-Slash"* is based on a campfire story my cousin, Shannon, told me and my cousins one night at my grandparents' house in Stillwell, OK. I created a lore and backstory for the evil legend – and using real towns in Eastern Oklahoma as settings. I got it published in 2001 on a defunct website, 31eyes.com, and again a couple of years ago in the anthology, **"Children of the Dead: Lost Lullabies."**.

"Slish-Slash v. The Union and Confederacy" came from a random line in the original story when I wrote about how she killed a bunch of Union and Confederate soldiers in one night. It's a little preachy, as it was written as the Iraq War was going on and our nation was becoming divisive (although that was pale compared to today).

"The Ballad of Sadie Blackheart" was needed because

what's a legend without a ballad poem to pass down to the generations? Even Freddy Krueger had "1, 2, Freddy's coming for you …"

"The Night the Devil Called a Radio Christian Talk Show" was hatched in the late 1990s. Although dated, I kept it in that time frame for context and to reflect the Evangelical Culture of that time. It's probably the most direct Christian Horror Story I wrote because it is about how easy it is for the Devil to use Christians with good intentions for his purposes. The main character is inspired from a real former radio evangelist who used (and still uses) sensationalism to promote himself instead of God.

"Dangerous Tonight" is also an unpublished work from 1985. I wrote it after seeing a movie about vampires and it has a somewhat similar premise to the 1987 movie, "Lost Boys." Since it was dated, it went through a rewrite about three years ago to update the times, although the story still remains. Pay attention to the main character because he will be in the second book of my *"Blind Faith Trilogy."* Also, it is named for an Alice Cooper song (I just hope he doesn't sue me.) This one's dedicated to my friend, Alex Edwards.

Sweet dreams!
Stephen W. Scott

NIGHT OF THE CROWS

The scarecrow stared at Jackson. The burlap head had jagged cuts with hideous stitches crisscrossing its jaws. The eyes, dark like caverns, were set back underneath its forehead. A few stitches draped across the irregular rectangular sockets. The mouth, also cavernous, was stretched wide with a few stitches across the opening, making it look as if it had teeth. The hat's brim tried to hide the evil face. The stiff, long, outstretched arms loomed over the boy, looking as if they were ready to pull him closer. The overalls and dark shirt were both tight, stuffed with branches and hay. A black, oversized, long coat flapped. Boots dangled from the pants, making it look like it had real legs and feet. The wind bounced them off the base of the wooden stake.

Jackson sensed a vile hatred as an intense fear bubbled in his chest. Cold, sharp pinpricks pushed on his insides – radiating clockwise around his heart and lungs – spreading like a twister's damaging winds. The scarecrow had a vile hatred for him. Why?

"What's up, bro?"

Jackson's joints flexed and his heart jumped out of rhythm for a split second at the touch and voice of his older brother. "Jesus! Michael." He sighed angrily. "Knock it off."

Tauntingly, he whispered into Jackson's ears. "It's gonna getcha. While you're asleep. It'll crawl through the cornfields, up to your window and ..."

"Shut up," Jackson said, pushing Michael away. He glanced at the lifeless scarecrow, wondering if it merely watched ... waiting for the right moment to spring to life, jump off the pole, and pounce on them.

"Why are you so spooked over a stupid scarecrow?"

"It's scary."

"Grandma says dinner'll be ready in ten minutes." He shook his head then sang quietly. "If I only had a brain ..." The tall stocks of corn quickly swallowed sight and sound of Michael.

Keeping his eyes on the scarecrow, he moved out of the small clearing back to the house. The circling fear faded with distance – but never fully disappeared. Several cackles erupted from some crows – calling the anxiety to rush back. Jackson stopped, wondering why the crows belted out so many 'caws.' Everything inside stilled as a crow let out a dying cry. Still, his neck snapped back and forth several times – wonder if he should go back and see what happened to the bird.

He turned, going back to the scarecrow. The fear circled up in his chest again, carrying a cold terror. His heart thumped faster, becoming painful. Or did his heart pump slower? His stomach wrenched on itself, becoming a tight knot.

As Jackson found the clearing, the scarecrow's face appeared. Its hateful, taunting smirk intimidated him. Was there more hay near the scarecrow's stake? Wasn't the head tilted to the left? Wasn't the top button on its shirt secure before? Dropping to one knee, he noticed crow feathers on the ground. Small droplets of blood covered the hay straws.

The head slowly moved to the right. Jackson yelped, fell backwards, and kicked at the stake. The scarecrow's head jerked to a stop on the shoulder then fell forward, resting its chin on the chest. Jackson clutched his chest as if trying to keep his heart from beating too fast. He realized that the wind merely carried the head over.

Standing, Jackson kept an eye on the monster. He lost breath, froze, and narrowed his eyelids. Near the mouth, a few black feathers seemed stuck. Also on the sack material, he noticed a few drops of blood. The wind and the rustling leaves faded into oblivion as he focused on the scarecrow.

His fear did not go away. It mounted, forcing him to turn away and get back to the house. However, after a good number of steps – Jackson froze. *Is something watching me.* He walked again. *Is something following me?* He stopped, trying to capture the sound of another set of footsteps. Nothing. Had the footsteps stopped, too? He wanted to run, but for some reason, he kept still. He took another step, then another. Soon, he resumed at a normal pace. The second set of footsteps returned. He stopped, trying to isolate them. They stopped, too. Or had they really been there in the first place? He felt strange eyes piercing his back.

Biting his lower lip, Jackson kept telling himself the scarecrow could not follow him. It had no bones for structure or muscles to move. The hay and cotton would provide no strength for either the legs or the arms.

A powerful, irrational fear conquered all reason and logic. Feeling trapped, scared, and uncertain, he walked faster. Unable to catch the extra steps out of sync with his, Jackson walked as fast as he could.

They jumped up at him, shrilling loudly. Catching only a glimpse, Jackson screamed, ducked, and covered his head as they moved towards his eyes. Their flight generated a slight breeze, and a talon scraped his hand.

Realizing the apparitions were nothing more than crows, his breathing returned to normal, and his heart stopped racing ... until a crow let out a dying caw. Jackson bolted back to the house.

***

Jackson fought against the annoying song as he poked at his food. He kept glancing out the window, hoping to catch sight of the scarecrow.

"Whatcha lookin' for, son?"

Examining his grandfather, he took notice of the tan, distinguished wrinkles. Still, the rich eyes glowed with wisdom, pride, and strength. The partially bald head was only protected by a few silver comb-overs. "What's wrong?"

Jackson stammered. Grandpa would think Jackson was nuts. Still, unable to hide his fear and curiosity, he had to ask. "Grandpa," he said quietly, "when did you get that old scarecrow?"

Grandpa hesitated. He looked as if he either thought hard ... or tried to hide something. "That scarecrow ... was there when my father bought the farm. We'd fix it up, patch holes, get fresh burlap sacks, stuff new hay into it. Dad and I had a lot fun doing that." He took a bite. "Why do you want to know?"

"Well..." He hesitated, fearing rejection—or perhaps laughter, as opposed to sympathy.

"Grandpa," said Michael, "Jackson's afraid of it."

"Shut up!" Jackson tried to kick Michael but missed.

"Well," said Grandpa, "that is a frightening scarecrow. Scariest one I ever seen."

"It looks evil ... like it's trying to scare something more than the crows away."

Grandpa took another bite of his dinner and shook his head. "Nope. It's just there for the crows."

***

Jackson strode through the corn stalks. The angry wind whipped through the tall corn. Some leaves and stems clicked together; others slapped his face. Was he crazy going back alone? Was that scarecrow angry at him? Was it after him? No. The whole idea was ridiculous. Finally, the stalks spread as the scarecrow's shadow covered him.

Gawking at the scarecrow, he swallowed so hard it almost hurt. Tilting his head, he examined it closely. The mouth seemed wider, and the eyes appeared more slanted. *No, it's not any different from yesterday.* Or was it? He moved closer, wanting to touch it and prove it was nothing more than a pair of overalls stuffed with hay. Fearful, he hesitated. What if it grabbed him? Or maybe tried to bite him?

Jackson took a deep breath and climbed the ladder, almost face-to-face with it. Ready to jump down, he cringed. His arm stretched. His hand extended. His fingers cowered for several seconds, then he jabbed its chest. It folded under the force of three fingers. Shoving it with his hand, he tried to provoke a reaction. Nothing. He reached closer to the mouth. He quivered putting his fingers, hand and left arm down its mouth. Was that a mannequin head he felt?

He relaxed and pulled his arm out of the scarecrow's mouth. Disappointed, he wondered why it did not attack. He examined the dry blood near its mouth. After rubbing it, he wondered if it was blood— or something else.

Caw! Caw! Caw!

The crow startled him. Again, he did not know if the crow tried to scare him or warn him. Jackson turned and walked away. The wind cut through the cornfield, rattling the leaves. He hurried, almost running through the stalks. The wind stopped, stilling not just the corn crop, but also Jackson. Soft footsteps circled him. His head turned sharply, trying to find the strange eyes. "Grandpa?" Jackson did not wait long for a reply. "Michael?" He kept turning, watching for the stalks to bend. The footsteps got closer ... and slower. Biting his lower lip, he flexed his legs to stop them from shaking. Sweat poured incessantly from his forehead and palms. "Leave me alone. Please. I won't tell anyone. I promise." He repeated the whisper a few more times. Part of him wanted to see the scarecrow to be sure the thing came to life to prove himself right – or did he want to prove himself wrong?

Something moved behind him. He jerked his head but only saw corn ears and leaves sway several times, showing a trail, but not revealing his tormentor.

Ten or maybe twelve crows erupted into a cacophony of caws again. They sounded dangerous, ominous, or angry. Covering his ears, he backed away from the noises. The crows did not stop. His panic exploded into a run. Pushing aside leaves, he hoped the crows might lose him ... or at least shut up. Corn plants came alive, trying to grab or trip him.

Something latched onto Jackson's face, arms, and legs. He tried to stop, but at full speed continued forward until the invisible, but powerful shield reached its maximum stretch. Bouncing, it yanked him back, knocking him to the ground. Finally seeing the barbed wire, he felt the tiny, painful holes in his body.

The crows stopped. One let out a dying gasp – leaving a deathly stillness and blunt dread. Only conscious to the sound of his own breathing, he moved through the cornfield back towards the scarecrow. The journey seemed to take only a few seconds. The closer he approached the scarecrow, the worse he felt. His stomach tensed. His heart beat a strange, erratic rhythm.

"If I only had a brain ..." Jackson closed his eyes, hoping to find some courage ... and blot out the ridiculous song. At the clearing, he gawked at the lifeless scarecrow. Jackson stooped, seeing a beak, part of a neck, and a few black feathers near the foot of the wooden stake. Blood stained the straw and leaves. Jerking his head up, he caught sight of blood near the scarecrow's mouth. The hands! They had some feathers, and a talon. Cold pinpricks swirled in an eddy, spreading through his insides. He wanted to run, but remained still, staring deeply into the scarecrow's black eyes.

The scarecrow subtly lifted its head then turned to face Jackson. Staring at its eyes, he knew a darkened soul possessed the inanimate object. The fear sliced into Jackson's soul then pushed him to run as fast as he could.

***

The song inside Jackson's head changed. Although it was still to the tune from the song in The Wizard of Oz, the pleasant music was replaced with harsh strings and dissonant sounds as a low, coarse voice sang the lyrics that flowed into Jackson's mind:

If I strayed from this stake/whether you're asleep or awake/and you're feeling fear and shame/I'd find a nice sharp sickle/ believe me it would not tickle/as I'd slice out your little brain/ I'd unravel you to tears/make you quake in fears/and drive you insane/ I'd find no remorse-us/as I sang another chorus/ while slicing out your little brain.

Frightened, chilled, Jackson turned on his side away from the window. He used his pillow, trying to blot out the horrible song. Clamping his eyes tight, he tried to hold back his tears. His stomach tightened. He knew the scarecrow was alive. Possessed. It wanted to hurt him.

Jackson wondered how it could grab the crows without getting off the stake? How could it move with only hay for a body? It would have no strength. How could it eat the crow without teeth ... or a stomach? It did not make sense. It was not possible! Irrational fear, again, defeated all logic.

What could he do? No one would believe him. If they did believe him, how would they help him? Helpless, a dark dread draped over him.

The outside wind picked up, howling off the outside gutters and other objects. It sounded like a banshee wailing a death song. A slight remnant of the cold seeped through. He shook as his throat tightened. A freezing cold started at his stomach and spread. The song, marred in a low, demonic voice, repeated. He almost cried.

His fear was interrupted as he tried to remember what the lion sang in the movie. The girl wanted a home. The tinman wanted a ... heart. What did the lion sing? The question kept him awake. At least his mind was not on the scarecrow.

He winced, hearing something scrape the window screen. He turned back to his other side, wanting to keep an eye on the door and window. His heart stilled, losing his breath. He remembered the tree outside. One branch always scraped the screen in high winds. Hesitating, he slowly pulled the covers off and sat up on his bed. He stared at the window, listening to the sound.

Scrape, scrape, scrape.

With his eyes fully adjusted to the dark, Jackson stared at the drawn curtains. He kept reminding himself that the sound was nothing more than the old tree branch that annoyed him many times in the past. He finally stood—moving closer towards the curtains. He yanked them open. The branch scraped the screen. He relaxed.

Jackson's whole body had one huge muscle twitch as the scarecrow jumped at his window. Its arms tried to push through the glass. Its mouth moved strangely, as if trying to speak. After the freezing cold ran through his stiffened body, his fear erupted into a yell and he fell backwards.

The lights came on as Grandma and Grandpa rushed in. "What is it?"

Jackson pointed at the window, "The scarecrow! It's alive and it's after me! It's right..." Fear turned to embarrassment as he stared at his own reflection in the window. Rushing forward, he looked out the window, trying to find the scarecrow.

"You are such an idiot," said Michael.

Jackson ignored his brother and kept looking for the scarecrow. No longer scared, he felt foolish.

"Get out of here and back into bed," Grandma said to Michael.

"Son," said Grandpa, "you just had a bad dream. That's all."

Jackson kept staring at the window, strangely hoping it might come back. Embarrassed to look at his grandparents, he mumbled. "I'm sure I saw it. I could've sworn..." Maybe they were right, and he dreamt it.

Grandma put her arms around him, escorting him back to bed. "Do you want to sleep with a light on?"

"I'm 11, Grandma. I don't need a light." He sighed. "I'm sorry."

"Don't apologize for a nightmare, boy. It's not your fault," said Grandpa as he closed the curtains.

The light vanished. The hall illumination silhouetted Grandma's shining face. For the first time, he noticed the similarity between Mom and Grandma's eyes. He missed Mom and Dad. Perhaps the shock of their death a few weeks ago stressed his fears.

"Grandma … I love visiting you, but I've always been scared of that scarecrow because of how ugly and evil it was. Now I have to live with it." A tear escaped.

Grandma smiled, leaned closer and kissed Jackson on the forehead. She left the door slightly ajar. He stared at the light that beamed through the door crack. Maybe the light would frighten the scarecrow away.

Jackson sat up. That's what the lion sang! The Cowardly Lion needed the nerve ... courage ... bravery. *If I only had the nerve.* Staring at the closed curtains, he realized he needed the same gumption as the lion. Refusing to be afraid, he stood, determined to stop the scarecrow.

⁂

Jackson's eyes scanned back and forth. A wind rushed through him, chilling his skin, and making him shake. He turned his head to keep the dust, leaves, and any other debris out of his eyes. He shined his flashlight at the cornfield.

The barn doors rattled and slammed. The wind? He sauntered towards the barn and peered through the door, scanning the inside with his flashlight. Farm equipment hung from hooks and ropes. Some wind seeped through the boards and holes, causing the tools to gently click together, and cast strange, bizarre shadows from the outside light and full moon.

Setting the flashlight on a table, Jackson found some rags and some kerosene. He poured the fuel on the rags then tied them to a large stick. He hoped the scarecrow would be afraid of fire like the one in the movie. He kept looking over his shoulder, hoping it did not pounce on him. Finding the matches, he lit the torch. The wind tried to extinguish the flames, but they stayed alive.

Jackson closed the barn door, latched it shut, then turned to the cornfield. As the light danced across the tall stalks, shadows crisscrossed and converged, covering everything like a blanket. He hesitated, knowing it waited for him.

He moved the torch carefully so as not to set anything ablaze. He wondered where the scarecrow waited. He took a deep breath before yelling, "I know you're out there," his quivering voice tried to be strong. "And I'm not afraid."

Footsteps rushed behind him, fading quickly. He turned sharply, looking for the monster. "Okay," he whispered, "I lied. I'm scared to death."

Caw! Caw! Caw!

Jackson tensed, feeling as if his spirit had jumped to escape his body. He turned towards the sound. He screamed at the sight of long arms reaching for him. The scarecrow's expression changed to shock as some flames caught its forearm. It patted the flames and scurried away. Jackson's breaths raced, almost hurting his chest. Paralyzed, he stared at the darkness for a few more seconds.

Caw! Caw! Caw!

His bones, muscles, and skin twitched – almost allowing his spirit to escape again. Jackson caught a glimpse of the scarecrow's face. It glanced at the wounded arm, then at him. It moved out of the light's range. The footsteps circled Jackson. Frantic, he searched for the scarecrow.

The kerosene smell faded as the torch's flames faded. *No! Not now!* The fires, exhausting their fuel, dwindled to nothing. Frightened, hopes dashed, he knelt, hoping to figure out a way to rekindle the fire. Nothing came to mind. Jackson felt for his flashlight.

Sticks scraped his skin. Strong, dry hands wrapped around his neck. Jackson pulled away as the flashlight ignited. Spinning around, he clubbed the scarecrow's head. Not solid, he hit it harder, hoping to knock the hay loose.

His flashlight shined at the looming scarecrow. Its long coat flapped in the wind, making. A subtle red light emanated from its eyes. Picking up its hat, the scarecrow put it back on. Its arms extended through the sleeves. The gloved hands grabbed Jackson's neck and retracted.

Jackson panicked, kicking and hoping to find ground. Grunting, trying to find breath, he kicked his legs and tried to find the ground. He hit its elbows. The sticks did not feel that strong, but no blow broke them. Jackson felt the strain in his neck and spine.

The scarecrow's mouth widened. It spread four, perhaps six inches wide. The cavernous mouth had burlap stitches turning into jagged teeth. The smell reminded him of the dung heap behind the barn, mixed with moldy, rotting vegetables. The mouth opened wider.

Almost crying, he remembered the flashlight in his other hand. He tried to use it and hit the scarecrow on the head. Its arm blocked the blow, scraping Jackson's hand and forcing him to drop it.

Jackson's head, almost inside the scarecrow's mouth, pounded within. Dizziness rushed through his brain, and his vision blurred. Consciousness ebbed. His legs stopped kicking.

Three crows shrilled as they descended at the scarecrow's head. A third sank its talon into the scarecrow's arm and it pecked at the head. More crows descended, attacking the monster with their beaks and talons.

Jackson hit the ground. The jarring forced a cough. His mouth heaved in all the air it could. After four or five breaths, he recovered the flashlight and pointed it at the scarecrow. It grabbed one crow and ripped the bird's body apart and ate it. The two others descended again, knocking off its hat. The birds took turns dropping, pecking, and scraping it with their talons. The scarecrow finally caught one, ripped it apart and ate it.

Although he almost tripped on a few stalks, he managed to run. He kept his footing. Some stalks slapped his face. He ran a few more feet and stopped. Which way was the house? He looked frantically for some light to show the way. None existed. Feeling trapped in the dark cornfields, he did not know what to do.

Caw! Caw! Caw!

Jackson ran towards the hideous chorus that erupted everywhere. The sounds chilled his skin, muscles, and bones. For some reason, he ran towards them, hoping they might be telling him the way. The sounds stopped as he broke through the edge of the cornfield. He halted at the sight of all the crows. None of them flinched as he scanned them with the flashlight. Scared, he backed up, getting closer to the cornfield.

The scarecrow's hands grabbed Jackson's neck. His throat crushed under the grip. Again, his vision faded, and his thinking faded to sleepiness. The crows erupted into flight while cawing. The scarecrow let go. The boy coughed his breath back. He felt their feathers, talons, and beaks brush by, chasing the scarecrow. Jackson followed. Reaching the other end of the cornfield, his flashlight captured the sight. The murder descended on the scarecrow. They pecked at it with their beaks and scratched it with their talons. The monster tried to push them away, but too many descended too fast. Finally, one arm fell apart as the fabric was torn and hay, cotton, and sticks spilled. The face collapsed as another crow tore it open. More hay fell, along with a large mannequin head. The crows relented, landing either on the barbed wire or the ground. Silent, they all looked at Jackson. Almost as if taking turns, they scattered.

***

A rooster crow woke Jackson. Remembering the night before, he glanced outside to see the scarecrow still in pieces. He wondered what made it come alive, and what made the crows attack it.

"Jackson," yelled Grandma, "go out to the barn and tell your grandfather to come in for breakfast."

He got dressed and went outside. Still somewhat dark, Jackson poked his head inside. A kerosene lamp outlined Grandpa's figure. He mumbled to himself.

"Grandpa, Grandma says come in for breakfast."

"I'll be there in a minute. Damn crows tore apart my scarecrow and drug it to the edge of the fence."

Jackson pretended not to know anything. He closed the door, leaving Grandpa alone.

Grandpa worked hard on a new scarecrow. Stopping, he wondered if the scarecrow really went after Jackson. It should have only taken care of the crows. Determined, he worked furiously. He had to protect the main crop.

Looking over his shoulder, he made sure Jackson left. Pulling a small sheet of paper from his shirt pocket, he examined it. "I sure hope this spell makes this scarecrow stronger."

Caw! Caw! Caw!

Grandpa glanced at the lone crow in the barn. "Damn birds."

22

PUMPKIN LIGHT

A guttural growl shot across the darkened room. Flashlights converged on a hideous beast. No eyes, a crumpled nose, and a mouth hidden behind a thin veil of flesh—the beast charged.

Sam, unable to scream, tried to run, but only tripped over a blanket and pillow. Hitting the wall, he toppled on his cousin. She screamed, adding to his fright. He pushed her aside and tried to escape the monster's reach.

The lights came on. Laughter and smiles eased Sam's fears. The monster pulled the panty hose off its head. He sighed, seeing Uncle Drew. Gasping, he tried to catch his breath. "You … you … really scared me."

"Sam, you're such a weenie," said Cody.

"Now, son, you were running just as fast," said Uncle Drew.

"But he was so funny," Cody said while laughing.

Sam glared at his cousin. "No funnier than you …"

"Boys," Uncle Drew said while stepping between them, "it's just a Halloween scare. Knock it off."

"Dad," said Cody, "can we carve a Jack-O-Lantern?"

"Sure," he said. "We need Sam to show us how to do this."

Aunt Connie had the pumpkin ready. Uncle Drew carved the top and removed it. Cody and Sam worked hard at removing the innards. Hard to grasp, Sam struggled to remove the slimy, sticky, messy gunk. Although gross, they kept at it until it was all pulled out.

After washing their hands, Sam turned to face the pumpkin. Uncle Drew approached it with a knife. "No," he said, "my dad taught me how to do this. You gotta do it a certain way – or it won't work."

"Work? Jack-O-Lanterns can't work – you idiot." said Cody.

"My dad said if you don't make them right, they won't stop the evil spirits."

"You don't believe that junk, do you?"

Sam gritted his teeth, determined not to cry. "It's just what Dad said. Okay."

Uncle Drew put his arm around Cody. "Let him do it his way, son."

Sam worked hard. He drew the eyes slanted—with the corner of the eyes pointing away from the face. While the nose simply was an upside-down triangle, the mouth had a more ominous look. The teeth were jagged and offset, looking as if they could actually bite. Meticulously, he cut out the shapes, sculpting them perfectly. Mesmerized by the task, he lost track of time.

"Ooh, that's scary," said Aunt Connie.

"It has to be," he whispered. "It has to keep the evil spirits away." He put the candle inside then lit the wick. Sam felt the heat of the flame as he put the top on like a lid. Touching the outside of the pumpkin, he traced the cool surface—following the grooves.

The lights disappeared. The orange pumpkin light flickered strangely, almost dancing across the walls. Suzie, Sam's younger cousin, hugged her Mommy, obviously scared of the hideous beast. Cody came closer to the Jack-o-Lantern, almost hypnotized. "That's the freakiest, scariest one I've ever seen," whispered Cody. "How'd you learn to do that?"

"My dad."

* * *

Sam turned away from the pumpkin, looking at the wall filled with a dancing, orange light. The pumpkin light's outline on the wall seemed frightening. The sharp, angry, eyes winked maniacally. The teeth formed a jagged, ominous shadow that looked as if they moved.

Closing his eyes, he found it unsettling that the hideous image remained perfect in his mind. Opening his eyes one more time, he glanced at the last picture of himself with Mom and Dad. They took the picture at Niagara Falls – just a few weeks before they died. Liking that image much better, he closed his eyes and sought a pleasant dream.

The silence lulled him to bliss. Almost asleep, he

lost a sense of reality. Something cold pricked his skin. Tingling, yet painful, something grated on his shoulder. All the heat left his body. Feeling trapped, scared, his insides shrank—as if a huge weight tried to crush his soul. Unable to breathe, Sam forced his eyes open. A dreadful fear loomed over him. His jaw quivered and he shook.

The pumpkin light startled him. The orange glow of the mouth did not merely dance but rather moved up and down as if the Jack-O-Lantern came to life and tried to speak. The triangular eyes widened then narrowed as if angry. Turning sharply while sitting up, he faced the pumpkin. It looked just like it did before he finished carving it.

Sam continued to stare at the pumpkin as the warmth returned to his body. He stopped shaking. A dead stillness cast its own uncertain, dark fear. Almost hypnotized by the glowing pumpkin light, he stood from his bed and slowly approached the Jack-O-Lantern. Quickly, he expelled all the air from his lungs and extinguished the flame. The pumpkin light disappeared, rendering everything dark.

***

Sam cringed as the warm water hit his back. Turning his torso, he hoped the shower would pull him fully awake. Fiery pain sensors resonated from his shoulder. Grunting, he pulled his trunk away from the hot, streaming water. Cursing lightly under a grunt, he clutched his shoulder while backing away from the shower spray. Looking at his flesh, he noticed the punctures near his shoulder. Out of the shower, he examined the wound more closely in the mirror. His fingers moved across the puncture wounds, noticing a strange, yet definite pattern. It looked like a bite mark. He wondered how it got there – then remembered his dream. *Did the Jack-O-Lantern bite me?*

***

Feeling the cold brick wall against his back, Sam stared dead-eyed into Mark Haskins. His punch landed perfectly on Mark's nose. Enjoying the power, he shoved the boy into the other wall and delivered more punches. A few kids cheered him, but he did not hear them as he vented his rage on the class bully. Finally, a teacher pulled him off, agitating his tender shoulder. "Get off me!" he kept yelling.

"Listen young man," said the burly gym teacher as he shoved Sam into the chair, "you sit right there until I call your parents!"

"My parents are dead, you idiot!" A tidal wave of sadness billowed high, pushing out the anger along with a few tears.

Coach Wills paid no attention to Sam's anger. Soon, the principal and coach came back, asking him stupid questions. "Why did you hit him?" "What's going on with you?" "Why didn't you get a teacher to help?"

Reaching the age of eleven, Sam used the old stand-by response to all questions: "I don't know."

Adults obviously forgot the law of the playground: If you lay down before a bully, they walk over you. If you go tell a teacher, you're a rat and the bully will retaliate. And if you fight back, you get in trouble. It was a no-win situation.

Soon, Aunt Connie and Uncle Drew arrived. Sitting down with the principal, he knew the consequences. "I am going to suspend Sam for two days."

The drive home was quiet. He refused to answer Uncle Drew's quiet, yet stern questions. "Look, son, I know you're having trouble with your parents .."

"I'm not your son! So, stop trying to be my dad!" Unable to look at his aunt or uncle throughout dinner, a simmering anger festered – although he could not find either purpose or direction for his fury.

After dinner, he opened his textbook to do the homework assignment. The cryptic numbers did not make any sense. Sam struggled – trying to figure out how to multiply compound fractions. Of all the subjects at school, he hated math the most. Finding something to finally focus his anger, he slammed down his pencil.

Striking a match, Sam lit the candle inside the pumpkin. As the light spread from the carved object, the evil smile seemed to spread. A strikingly cold chill froze his skin. He felt slightly dizzy. The air was still. The orange eyes seemed to wink at him amidst the flickering flame. For a second, Sam wondered about the bite on his shoulder. How did it get there? What bit him?

"Boo!"

Sam jumped, then shoved his cousin.

"Hey," Cody said angrily, "I'm not only older, but I can also kick your little ass."

"I'd like to see you try!" Sam and Cody quickly locked in battle – grabbing each other like amateur wrestlers. Falling against the wall, Cody pushed back, knocking them into the flickering pumpkin light.

Cody froze – as if seeing something monstrous. A yell got caught in his throat. Bellowing forward, Cody grasped his mid-section. "What did you do to me? Dad! Dad!"

Shocked, Sam stared at his cousin – then at the flickering light that surrounded Cody.

"What is it?" asked Uncle Drew.

"Sam hurt me. We were fighting and … jeez – this hurts!"

Aunt Connie lifted Cody's shirt. Indentations covered Cody's stomach and back. Although no blood oozed from the wounds, Sam thought they looked like a bite.

"That's it, young man," Uncle Drew said sternly while pointing at Sam. "I was going to ground you for a week, but now it's two."

"But I …" Shocked, he tried to defend himself. "I didn't do it." He tried to explain what really happened. His mouth hung open, locked in place. Surely no one would believe him. Alone, he stared at the menacing Jack-O-Lantern. The eyes definitely winked at him—almost tauntingly. Hypnotized, the boy stared at the evil pumpkin.

After standing frozen for a few minutes, he stepped closer, feeling the flame's heat. Ironically, he felt cold inside. Shaking, nervous, the air felt quiet and stale. He lifted the top of the pumpkin and snuffed out the flame. He turned off the lamp, stripped to his underwear and crawled in bed. Afraid to sleep, he stared at the pumpkin's silhouette, hoping it did not spring to life and attack.

****

Sam's sleep stirred. Feeling cold, nervous, he felt something amiss. Fully awake, his eyes bolted open. He stared at the orange pumpkin light that danced across his wall. Shocked, his head turned sharply towards the Jack-O-Lantern. The flame burned strong again – casting an ominous life of its own. An uneasy quiet added to the growing dread. The anxious, dreary fright fell through his stomach, dragging his soul in its wake.

He shivered. His shortened breath was visible. He distinctly remembered blowing out the candle. He tried convincing himself this could not be real—or that he did not fully extinguish the flame with his breath. Stepping closer, he thought the mouth seemed wider, and that a few extra teeth had grown. Carefully, slowly, he inched his fingers closer to the mouth. *This is nuts*, he thought. *No, it's more nuts to think a pumpkin is alive.* Irrational fear kept him from inserting his fingers. All logic and reason compelled him to follow through. He slightly inserted his middle finger then withdrew it quickly. Focused on the large teeth, Sam inserted his hand just past the knuckle.

The Jack-O-Lantern's face contorted, raising its upper jaw. Frozen, Sam could not react as the teeth clamped down on his skin. Screaming, he tried to pull it back, but the Jack-O-Lantern's teeth meshed hard, trying to tear off his hand. The pain shot through his skin like a fire, then vibrated up his arm, feeling as if it were crushed.

***

Sam's eyes opened. His breath raged out of control, hurting his chest. Still in bed under the covers, he clamped his jaw tightly to alleviate the shakiness. Pain resonated from of his hand and up his arm. Turning on the small light next to his bed, he examined his skin. He cursed, seeing the teeth marks. Terrified, his fingers shook as a cold sweat drenched his skin. Fortunately, the wounds did not bleed, but the pain resonated like an insect sting.

An icy chill fell down his spine – seizing his heart and mind. He noticed the pumpkin light dance on his wall. The mouth moved up and down and the eyes widened. Sam's raging breath stopped as he stared at the shadowy picture. He turned his head sharply. The Jack-O-Lantern did not move. It grinned at him like a

31

Cheshire Cat. The eyes glowed. *Impossible*, he thought. *I blew out the candle before going to bed.* Maybe he did not blow it all the way out. Perhaps there was enough of a flame to simmer, and it re-light the wick.

He stood. Hesitant, scared, he moved closer to the pumpkin. The fear curled up into a ball of shock. Hesitantly, he moved closer. He took a deep breath and held it. Pulling in more air, he wanted to make sure to blow it out. With one contraction, he released the force of his breath through his lips. The blast snuffed the flame. A small veil of smoke seeped through the eyes and nose. In total darkness, he stared at the pumpkin's shadowy head.

The Jack-O-Lantern seemed to open its eyes as the flame slowly resurrected. Awakening from its slumber, the pumpkin emitted its orange glow once again. He released another breath, trying to snuff the flame. Again, the light retreated, then slowly returned. Stupefied, he wondered what to do with the Jack-O-Lantern. Should he try to throw it out? What if it tried to bite him? Maybe he could put a blanket over the face and rob the flame of its oxygen.

Sam opened his window. The cold October air pricked his skin. Focused, determined, he carefully picked up the warm pumpkin—making sure to keep his hands away from it mouth. After pushing it out the window, he closed and locked it. The Jack-O-Lantern did not crack—nor did the candle's flame die. The pumpkin landed on its back, looking up at him. Its eyes slightly widened, then narrowed.

Backing from the window, he hastily closed the drapes and crawled underneath the covers. He pulled the blanket tightly over his head, hoping to hide from the evil eyes.

***

An annoying sound reverberated, stabbing Sam's ears. His arm wriggled free of his coverings then wormed its way out in search of the alarm clock. His fingers acted like sensors, dancing across the bedside table. His mind knew the first object was an empty can of soda. The next thing was the base of the lamp. Finding the alarm clock, he tried to use his fingers and hit the mute button. Unable to find it, and feeling the cord, he pulled hard. The noise ceased.

Wriggling his head freely, Sam grunted. Although grateful he fell asleep, he felt too groggy and tired. He wanted to stay home and …

Sam yelled as the Jack-O-Lantern smiled at him. It rested atop his chest of drawers where it was last night before he tossed it out the window. Although the candle's light was gone, its mere presence intimidated him. Again, he yelped as the door opened, and Aunt Connie walked in. "Get up, get up, get up," she said while putting some clean clothes at the foot of his bed. "I have to take you and Cody to school early today."

Sam kept watching the Jack-O-Lantern. Its eyes slowly moved to the left, subtly watching Aunt

33

Connie's every move. Would it bite her? Was it stronger now? Why did the candle go out? How was this … thing alive? How did it get back inside?

"I said to get out of that bed!"

His anger burst. "You're not my mom!"

Aunt Connie stopped abruptly, choking back her emotion. "Your mother was also my sister. And I miss her, too."

As she left the room, the pumpkin's eyes watched again. The mouth frowned slightly. The teeth grew sharper—and longer. Sam rushed to the pumpkin and picked it up. "You leave her alone!" he whispered to it. "And my cousin …" The mouth moved down quickly on his right thumb. The searing pain forced him to drop the pumpkin. It did not break or crack. Holding his thumb, he glared at it. Even without the candle lit, it radiated a malevolent aura.

"Okay," he whispered, "I'll put you back – but don't bite me again. Please." Carefully, he picked it up and set it on the chest. Nervous, he cleaned, got dressed, and wrapped an ace bandage around his hand. All the while, he kept an eye on his Jack-O-Lantern. It seemed to grin wider – as if it enjoyed casting fear on him. While eating breakfast, Sam knew he had to get rid of it.

***

Sam tried a new search on the Internet: Occult Powers Jack-O-Lanterns. He was surprised to see so many sites. Taking a gamble, he clicked on one. His

34

access was denied by the school filter system. Tired of the system continuously blocking his research, he hit the table and sighed.

"What are you doing?"

He stiffened, trying to close the site.

"Get your hand off the mouse," said Ms. Rains, the school librarian. He withdrew his hand and let her explore the previous sites he tried to access. After several clicks, she glared at him. "Jack-O-Lanterns? What do you want to know about Jack-O-Lanterns?"

"I found out about the Irish Myth of Jack – the guy that outsmarts the devil, but I was trying to find out if the lanterns were supposed to have any … magical powers to scare away evil spirits or something like that."

Ms. Rains sat next to him. "Why?

"There's this one," he hesitated, worried that Ms. Rains would think him foolish. "Some Jack-O-Lanterns have silly, goofy smiles, but some are scary. I was wondering why."

"Are there any Jack-O-Lanterns that scare you?"

He fidgeted. "There's this one …" again he balked, wondering how to approach the subject. "It's … it's one I made."

"You made it?"

He nodded. "My Dad taught me how to make them scary. He said if you made them right, they ward off evil spirits."

"Did you know that when many ancient peoples

like Native Americans and the ancient people of Sumera made a painting, carving, or statue, they believed it was inhabited by ancient spirits. Sometimes, they thought a part of their spirit inhabited their work of art."

"So, the Jack-O-Lantern is me?"

"Maybe just a little part of your personality, your soul. Have you talked to your dad about this?"

He shook his head, as if ashamed. "I can't. He died."

Ms. Rains closed her eyes, almost as if she shared Sam's pain. "I'm so sorry. How did he die?"

Sam did not want to cry, but a tear managed to stream down his left cheek. "He and my mom died in a plane crash. It was a small plane." He looked down, recalling the day when the police came to Uncle Drew and Aunt Connie's house. "I thought he was a good pilot. He promised to come back and I … I …" No longer embarrassed, needing to let loose the pain, he let out his tears. Sobbing, he hugged her tightly. Feeling her arms return the embrace, he savored the warm, friendly hug. For the first time in a while, he felt safe. After a few minutes, Sam pulled away from the hug. She handed him some tissue, and he dried his tears and blew his nose.

"Would you like to talk to the counselor?"

Sam shook his head while sniffing.

"How would you like to stay here and help me clean up?

Sam nodded.

***

"So, what are you going to dress up as for Halloween?"

Sam gulped hard as the Jack-O-Lantern cast its eyes on Uncle Drew. The orange light slightly flared – as if preparing to strike.

"Son, stop staring at the pumpkin and look at me when I talk …" Uncle Drew looked around, "Why is it so cold in here all of a sudden?"

"Uncle Drew," he hesitated, worried his uncle would think him nuts. "I … uh … I think … the Jack-O-Lantern is after me."

Uncle Drew looked perplexed. Sitting on the bed, he looked at the Jack-O-Lantern, then at Compassion radiated through his eyes as his voice softened, and his hands rubbed Sam's shoulders. "What makes you think that?"

He squirmed, then gulped hard. "I think it bit me—twice."

"I thought it was supposed to repel evil spirits?"

Embarrassed, he looked at the floor.

"Son," Uncle Drew said quietly, "maybe the Jack-O-Lantern is attacking something in your spirit."

"Like what?"

"Your anger."

"I don't understand."

Uncle Drew put his arm around Sam. "You're very angry, aren't you? You get into an argument with your aunt, fight with that boy at school and at Cody. Who are you angry with?"

Sam shook his head. "I don't know."

"Yourself? Your Mom and Dad? Maybe for leaving you?"

He noticed a few tears on his face. Uncle Drew pulled him tightly. Sam cried on his uncle's shoulder.

***

Sleep eluded Sam. Between the dreamscape and simple sleep, he stirred as his ears tingled. Listening, he heard the whispers – although they made little sense. Forcing his eyes open, he sensed a strange comforting calmness. Glaring at the Jack-O-Lantern, it glowed menacingly in the dark. At first, he tensed, but quickly found the soothing, comforting aura return. Two distinct shadows disrupted the orange pumpkin light. He tried to find the source, but it seemed something remained outside his vision. Turning, he tried to capture the presence in his room. Unafraid, the entities seemed familiar.

Smelling Mom's perfume triggered a slight smile. His hair fell under a warm, invisible weight. The unseen hand gently petted his head—just like Mom did so often. The other spirit had a quiet, deep bass voice. A strong, firm touch clasped his shoulder. Dad.

The pumpkin light dimmed as if robbed of oxygen. Soon, the flame vanished, leaving the Jack-O-Lantern a mere silhouette. The brief touches of spirits vanished. He wanted them back desperately. Still, he smiled,

38

enjoying the last few seconds.

Standing, he put on a robe, took the Jack-O-Lantern out and set it outside on the front porch. Staring at the pumpkin one last time, he gave it a kick. It rolled down the sidewalk then came to rest near a tree.

***

Mom's angry tirade echoed in Mark's ears. Now he had school. Neither was appealing for Mark Haskins. In fact, he did not know if he dreaded school more than home. School left a bitter, sour taste in his mouth, while home drowned his soul. He shoved his little brother, Robbie, to the side.

"Move it you little…" Mark could not finish his sentence as something knocked his foot away from solid ground. Falling, he heard laughter from his brother. He started to get up and chase his insolent sibling but came face-to-face with something grotesque. Mesmerized, Mark could not stop staring at the well carved, decaying Jack-O-Lantern. "Wow," he said quietly. "Look at this."

"That looks so evil," said Robbie.

"It's mine, now, butt-wipe." said Mark as he picked it up. Pain swelled in his foot, forcing Mark to limp. Did something bite his foot?

He stopped to look at the Jack-O-Lantern. A dying ember on the candle turned into a flame and started to grow.

TONGUES AFIRE

Jesse smirked, lifting the left corner of her mouth, and raising her left eye. Hearing her friends laugh made her proud. She towered over the crying girl who retreated to the chain link fence. Unable to contain herself, Jesse laughed heartily. It felt good as the new girl burst into tears and ran away.

A strong hand clasped her arm and yanked her away. "What'd you say to her?"

A quick whitewash and her innocent girl look returned. She hunched her shoulders. "Nothing."

"She's crying over nothing?" Miss Dennis turned to the other girls. Jesse didn't worry a bit. Laura, Shelly, Sara and Katy would never squeal. They thought of her as a god. She was God. Daddy always called her princess, which fueled her idea that she was above reproach. He would take care of this jerk.

The teacher yanked Jesse away from her friends, finally irritating her. "You're hurting me," she said, trying to pull away. "I'll tell my Daddy."

Miss Dennis pulled harder, "Great. It'll go fine with my report."

Jesse screamed a little, although she added some

flare intentionally so the other kids would see. Perhaps another teacher would spot the melee and interfere. Mr. Richards always took her side.

Laura quickly caught up. "We're witnesses! You can't touch her like that!" Shelly and Katy added their remarks to Miss Dennis. Again, Jesse felt untouchable, invincible as her friends came to her defense.

She resisted unsuccessfully, finding herself in the principal's office. Sitting down, she mimicked Mrs. Dennis, making cackling noises and shaking her head. If she could make her teacher come unglued, it would be worth it. As Ms. Dennis went into the principal's office, she glanced over at the new girl. She still sobbed heavily. Jesse's smile returned along with her elation. It was like a notch on her belt, or perhaps a medal of honor. She ruled the eighth grade and now the new girl knew it.

"Get in here," the burly principal did not scare her.

Her smirk returned, and she rolled her eyes at him.

"Get that damn look off your face and get in here now."

She stood defiantly. "You can't talk to me that way! I'll tell my Daddy."

"Go ahead and tell your daddy," said Mr. Dean. "I've had it with you. That poor little girl is crying because you think it's cute to spread rumors."

"I didn't say anything."

Ms. Dennis handed Mr. Dean a note. "Amanda gave me this before lunch."

Jesse's heart sank. Her warm elation turned cold and sank into her chest. Her shoulders hunched closer. Surely that little bitch didn't snitch on her. That letter was private between her and Amanda. She would pay for this. Perhaps a cell phone picture in the bathroom or in the locker room. A few postings on snapchat or TikTok would certainly show her.

Mr. Dean read the note aloud:

"'Amanda, you cannot even sit next to our table during lunch. The girls have already taken a vote and determined you are too ugly and cannot be in the circle. You look like a slut, or a lesbian. In any case, do the school a favor and die.'" Mr. Dean sighed. "And you signed it, too."

Her mind scrambled for some sort of excuse. Usually, one came to mind. However, now, a quick lie eluded her.

"Since this is bullying, I ain't givin' you Lunch Detention. Three days in the hole."

"Three days! You're out of your mind!"

"You wanna go for four?" asked Mr. Dean, "That could easily be arranged if you don't keep your mouth shut. You start tomorrow."

Jesse hated the hole. Actually, it was in-school-suspension, but the kids called it the hole – and then the teachers and administrators started referring to it that way. You could not talk, sleep, be on your phone, or listen to music. Seven hours of boredom and nothing. She recalled it once in the Seventh Grade, for a similar offense, but that was only one day. Three days!

Gritting her teeth, Jesse sighed hard and stood. She walked past Amanda, glaring at her with one eye. The earlier anger seemed pale compared to now. Like boiling water, the hate swelled and popped inside, begging to get out and scald Amanda's skin and hair. She would get her revenge.

***

Jesse hurried into Mr. Richard's room. She hoped to talk to him and get some sympathy. Surely, he would believe her because he always asked her to pass out papers, run errands to the office, and make copies for him. She figured it was because he had two sons but never had a daughter he could spoil. Sure, he was naïve about her and some of the other girls, but he was also a good, funny teacher who got her excited about math. Surely that was worth something. Maybe he could talk to Mr. Dean.

"Mr. Richards ..." Her heart sank, seeing an unfamiliar face.

"Who are you?"

"I'm Mr. Devlin. I'm filling in for Mr. Richards today. And you are ..."

"Jesse," she said quietly. Standing from the desk, she examined the substitute, wondering if he could be easily manipulated. He looked in his early 30's and very lean and handsome. His head was shaven, but his face was long enough to make him look very thin in the neck. His dark piercing eyes radiating an aura of confidence she admired. Sure, Mr. Richards was nice, but this guy was a dream. "Oh," he said, "Mr. Richards left me a note, saying you would help me."

She smiled as he looked directly at her. "He did?"

She sat down at her desk, watching him move around the classroom. Glancing down at his left hand, she smiled seeing no wedding ring. He could teach something dumb like Russian History, and she would not care. She imagined romantic words along with flowers, music, and expensive clothes. He would extend his credit limit just for her, living way beyond his teacher's salary.

She helped pass out the papers happily. Until … she saw Amanda. Her dreams faded amidst her hate that woke from its slumber. A slithering heat lifted inside, pushing higher and higher. Her stomach and chest tightened, working her fury closer to her heart. There, it felt strong, as if it could rip Amanda's own soul in half. Because of her she had to go to the hole for three days. *Well, I'm taking her with me.*

Getting back to her seat, her mind raced for a plot to get Amanda into the hole. Getting into a fight would not work because that would only add to her punishment. Pretending to be pushed might work. A vicious note. Yeah. Surely this chump would believe that. Sara sat behind Amanda, so it could work.

Her hands worked quickly, scribbling a note. She politely asked to sharpen her pencil. Walking by Amanda, Jesse carefully dropped the note between

Amanda's desk and the desk behind her. She made sure it landed on the floor noticeably. "Mr. Devlin," she said, "Amanda's passing notes."

He quickly moved from behind the podium to pick up the note. He read it aloud, "'Sara, I think this guy's an …' well I can't say that."

Jesse smirked when Amanda radiated a petrified look. She shook her head trying to deny the evidence. "I swear I didn't write the note."

"I know you didn't," said Mr. Devlin. He turned to Jesse. "You wrote it, didn't you?"

Unfazed, Jesse stuck to her lie. "But I saw her. Right there."

He picked up Amanda's journal. "But look, the writing is not the same."

Jesse hunched her shoulders and shook her head. "Well, she was passing it."

"It looks like the note you wrote earlier today. I saw it."

She almost felt naked. How could he know? She got punished right before this period. The warm anger turned to cold pin pricks on her skin. Her stomach dropped sharply. "But I …"

"Step outside," he said quietly.

She bit her lip as Mr. Devlin presented the note to her. "Why would you write something like that?"

Jesse let her anger come back. "Because I hate her."

"And hate works good, doesn't it?" he said moving

his head closer. "Keeps you warm and focused."

His strange whisper had a mystic allure. Her ears perked as he moved closer. "Yeah."

"Because she's your enemy. Your vice. A thorn in your side."

His voice stretched lower. The dark eyes moved closer—almost hypnotizing her. "Forget a dagger," he said, "or a gun. If you can hurt her with written or spoken words, it's more powerful, more hurtful. You don't harm flesh. You steal her soul."

Jesse smirked, captivated by his dark presence. The reckless force convinced her that this teacher was an outsider who tried to buck the system. He played by his own rules and did what he wanted. Moreover, what he said made sense.

"You've done it before. You show those girls who's in charge and who runs this show, right?"

"Yeah," she said, feeling his rebellious confidence enter her soul.

"She's evil and has to be stopped."

"Yeah."

"Jesse," he whispered, "have you looked into the eyes of evil?" A slithering cold sank through her chest into her belly. Freezing, her jaw quivered. Goose bumps ran through her arms. An empty, hollowed out feeling cascaded down her spine. Speechless, motionless, she watched Mr. Devlin hold up the note. "I can see what's in your soul." He folded it up and put it in his chest pocket. He smiled wickedly lifting only the left corner of his mouth, as well as his left eyebrow.

She went back inside to finish the day.

***

The bus ride seemed colder than usual. Sure, October temperatures fell dramatically in Colorado, especially close to the mountains. The cold wind, however, did not chill her more. It felt comfortable. Too comfortable. Used to it, she wondered why people from the south thought 40 degrees was cold. It was a walk in the park for someone from the north. A cold angry rain beat against the bus. She sat next to the heater, but it still felt too cold.

Tired, listless, Jesse shook her head, unable to wake up. Of course, she did not want to sleep. Last night, nightmares kept waking her. She tried hard to recall just one of the horrific dreams – but they lay just beyond her reach. A remnant of fear forced her limbs to shake slightly. She still felt goosebumps. They were not from the cold, but instead an unnerving dread. It made no sense. It penetrated deep beyond her skin, finding its way into her person.

The breaks squealed as the bus stopped. The sound reminded her of fingernails down a chalkboard. "Jesse," said Sara, "look who it is."

Amanda got on the bus with her brother. At least he was cute. The familiar hatred came back. She whispered to the girls across from her, "She blows her own brother."

Immediately, a fire spread in her mouth. Her

tongue felt like numerous wasp stings. Clutching her mouth, the pain spread to her teeth, gums, and the sides of her inner cheeks. It felt like her nightmare! As the pain swelled, subtle moans became audible. Breathing through her nose, she leaned back, praying the pain would go away. Finally opening her mouth, the heat escaped. The throbbing pain in her teeth stopped, as well as the stinging in her tongue.

"What's wrong?" asked Sara.

"That hurt."

"Are you okay? You look very pale."

"What?"

"You look like one of those goth people – except without the make-up. Here, look," she said, handing her a compact mirror.

Jesse lost a breath. Her eyes had a blank, emotionless glare. They seemed darker, lacking the powerful hue they usually had. Her skin appeared white, void of color and beauty. Her lips seemed bigger and also lacked color. Her hair fell in several directions as if it had not been washed for three or four days. What happened? *The boys won't think I'm gorgeous anymore.*

"Maybe I'm sick," she whispered.

Laugher caught her attention. Glancing back, Jesse saw Amanda talking with Brian. He was her boyfriend … or at least he was. They were still friends … sort of. He laughed as she talked. She smiled widely and flipped her hair back! Brian moved his face closer to hers. "She's moving in on Brian!" she whispered.

"So, what?" said Sara, "he broke up with you."

Jesse's eyes narrowed. "I won't let her get away with it. That little bitchy sl …" Immediately the fire returned to her mouth. The stings reverberated more this time. Panicked, she held her mouth and leaned forward. Why? What caused this? Her shortened breath almost whistled out her nose.

"Hey, if you're gonna be sick, don't throw up on me."

The pain faded quickly but left a remnant in the back of her throat. It dissipated slowly this time. Finally falling back, Jesse lifted her head and let go of her mouth.

"What's wrong with you?"

Unsure, uncertain, fearful, she lied. "I got a bad toothache."

***

Jesse sat in her dungeon. Actually, the cubicle had a desk. Ironically, it was like a tomb within a tomb. The hole had no windows. Only one door next to the teacher's desk led to the outside. There were ten cubicles, and each had a desk, not allowing any eye contact or conversation. The pale white walls resembled something out of an old hospital in dire need of repair. The lack of color disallowed any personality or individuality. Surely, this is what prison is like.

Having all her assignments, she glanced at Mrs. Reed. She monitored the students. A real teacher, all

49

the kids either assumed she screwed up and manned the hole as punishment, or that she was an incompetent teacher. Jesse could think of two or three other teachers who should have this duty.

Actually, the day seemed to go fairly fast. Jesse got her first and second period assignments done quickly. When she saw that barely one period had passed, she moaned. At least she got her work done. Usually, she only got half or a third of the assignment done in class. Frustrated, she tried to slow her pace. At least she brought a book to read.

Mrs. Reed focused on her computer. Seeing an opportunity, Jesse stealthily retrieved her cell phone from her backpack. Covering the speaker with her hand, she used her thumb to set it for text message. Maybe she could surprise Sara. Her fingers danced quickly across the buttons. What to say? "What's that bitch, Amanda doing with Brian?"

Unable to finish the message, the stinging burn exploded in her mouth again. Dropping the phone, she clasped her mouth. Why is this happening? What's going on? Curses echoed in her mind as the pain spread farther, faster, becoming more intense. It vanished as Mrs. Reed stood over her.

"What's that?" asked the teacher as she picked up the phone. "What's wrong with you?"

"A toothache," she said sheepishly.

Mrs. Reed took the phone and returned to her desk. She wrote something in her log. Surely it meant more days in the hole.   All because of that bitch …

Again, the fiery pain exploded. Jesse put one hand over her mouth and huffed through her nose. Tilting her head, she hoped to avoid Mrs. Reed's discomforting eyes. She kept hoping the pain would go away. The pain vanished—but slowly. Feeling normal again, Jesse moved her tongue around. It seemed all right. Her mouth, tongue, teeth, and gums had no burns. It seemed like her taste buds were fine.

Amanda.   Every time she said or thought something bad about her triggered the flames. Impossible. But it did happen twice on the bus, and just now when she just thought of her hatred. *That's crazy! No one will believe me. I don't believe it. I need a test.* Although determined, fright kept her at bay. Closing her eyes, she thought of wringing that little …

The pain this time forced her to hunch her shoulders and secrete saliva. The spit did not work. The fire raged out of control. The heat spread to the sides of her mouth, her throat—and she felt it underneath her nose. It finally subsided. Jesse tried writing something bad about Amanda. The shrill pain only let her get down one word. Again, she tried to hide the discomfort but failed. Once the pain faded, she realized nobody noticed.

Jesse realized the person she needed to talk to.

***

She had to hurry before the bus left. "Miss Dennis, do you know Mr. Devlin?"

51

"Who?"

"He substituted for Mr. Richards yesterday. He was the tall, good-looking teacher next door."

"If there was a good-looking single hot substitute like that next to my room, I would have remembered him."

She rushed next door and found Mr. Richards. "I don't know Mr. Devlin, Jess," he said. "Ask the office. They called him. They should know how to get a hold of him."

Mrs. McCarty, the office manager, seemed perplexed. "I don't recall meeting him yesterday morning."

"He substituted for Mr. Richards. I have to tell him something."

Mrs. McCarty kept looking at some papers. "You're thinking of someone else," she said, "I don't even have a Mr. Devlin on my substitute list."

The remaining hope faded, swirling into confusion. It almost hypnotized her. The feeling dropped into her stomach, emanating an apprehensive dread. He was here. She remembered him folding the paper and winking at her. A subtle, pulsing fear grew. It felt cold just like yesterday.

Laughter startled Jesse awake. Sara stood down the hall and pointed at her. Some other girls laughed again. She heard their whispers. "Zombie." She retreated from her friends. She sat alone on the bus— still feeling as if she was trapped in the hole.

***

Dr. Lucas grimaced. Sighing, he looked over at Jesse's parents. "I'm stumped. She has no fever, and her white and red blood counts are normal. She shows no sign of bacterial infection. I want to refer you to a dermatologist."

For the first time in days, Jesse felt an emotion other than dread. In the mirror, she looked ugly. Her skin still had a pale white hue. Her eyes looked almost dead. Although she washed it every day, her hair seemed as if it could never be clean. She felt worthless as Mom hugged her. She whispered in her ear. "You'll be fine. You'll be fine. We love you." Jesse felt some tears stream down her cheeks.

***

Jesse waved at Katy and Sara. They shook their heads and went towards the other end of the cafeteria. They couldn't do that to her. They had no right! Indignant, she picked up her tray, walked proudly over, and sat next to them. The light-hearted laughter and talking abruptly stopped. "What are you doing here?" Katy's words stung. They sounded so rude, hurtful, and arrogant.

Jesse tried to smile. She barely made her words audible. "I finally got out of the hole … I thought you'd be glad to see me."

Laura and Shelly did not even look at Jesse. Frozen, they stared at their food. Katy glared at Jesse, but she could not look at any of them any longer. She felt anger, bitterness, and hate scorching her skin – and it even singed her spirit.

"Jesse," Katy said angrily, "stay away from us. You're freaking us out."

Jesse tried to cry. The pit seemed to dry and isolated enough. This was worse. Unable to find any tears, she barely made her words audible again. "I thought we were best friends."

"You were wrong," said Katy, emphasizing "wrong." She stood and motioned for the other girls to follow. "Don't follow us."

"Goth went out about ten years ago," commented Laura.

Jess sat at the table alone. Nervous, scared, cold, she quivered. The shaking was in her shoulders, her arms, and jaw. Hunching her shoulders, she tried to find some sort of warmth. The fear permeated her soul, making her heart erratic, uneasy, and scared. She tried to surface a tear. It eluded her. Why? She felt like crying for days. No one can see me, she thought. Usually, she liked the attention from her drama. Now, it repulsed her.

She felt a presence next to her. Ashamed to look, afraid, Jesse trembled more. For a third time, she tried to cry but found no tears.

"Jesse?"

Finally seeing Amanda's eyes, Jesse shied away. Embarrassed, she tried to move away from her. Feeling a gentle clasp on her shoulder, Jesse started to pull away. She stopped, finding the warmth she sought for the last few days.

"Jesse, do you want to talk?"

Still ashamed, she could not look at Amanda's caring, pretty eyes. Was she jealous, or merely humiliated by the action? In either case, Jesse did not know what to do. Unable to strike back, or find any words, she kept quiet. Clearing her throat, she shook her head. "Why would you want to talk to me?"

"I thought you could use a friend."

Finally able to cry, Jesse felt warm again. Purging out, she leaned into Amanda's embrace.

***

Katy's words were quiet, but strong. "Obviously lesbians."

Laura and Shelly laughed.

"They deserve each other. Losers." Enjoying the laughter from Laura and Shelly added to Katy's worth. They hinged on every word. "They're both scum."

"My, my," said a voice, "what a wicked tongue."

Katy cringed as the shadow towered over her. Looking up, she tried to remember his name. The hypnotic stare had a forbidden, yet tempting allure. His voice, dark, confident, and sexy, excited her. "Mr. ….?"

"Devlin." He bent his knees to face them. "You girls enjoying your lunch?"

"Those were some very harsh words. Why did you say such things?"

"They're the truth," Katy said. She glared at Amanda and Jesse, casting her hatred towards them. "They're losers. They're evil."

He smirked, almost chuckling. It almost put Katy in trance. "Katy," he said, "have you looked into the eyes of evil?"

ANGRY HIGHWAY

"Get the hell out of the way!" Jerry made sure to honk twice at the fellow in the fast lane. The car moved over … slowly. He moved closer to the man's bumper and flashed his headlights. "Come on! Stupid jerk."

David clutched his armrest, trying to hide his fright. "Jerry. Calm down."

Jerry sped past the car. "What? You sidin' with that idiot? He was blocking the passing lane!"

David, hoping to dodge his trainer's blunt words, countered with a calm voice. "Well, you're almost 15 over the limit."

Jerry glared at David sternly. "I'm the professional here."

The trainee sighed, revealing his agitation.

"Do you wanna ride with me or not?"

Not liking the hostile tone, David sighed. "I just want to learn the procedures."

Jerry set the steering wheel between his legs, reached inside the bag and pulled out his hamburger. He ate it, then glanced at his newspaper.

David somehow hid his panic, reached over and took hold of the steering wheel.

"What the hell is wrong with you?" Jerry asked

through his bites.

"Just helping you out."

"I don't need your help. I do this all the time."

David released his grip and fought his own irritation at Jerry's tone. David was the new guy and wanted a job and certainly didn't want to piss off his trainer. He found a neutral subject. "So how long does the route take you?"

"Some days it's longer," Jerry said between chews. "Some days I have to go to Weatherford or Mount Vernon. It depends on what the physicians in those towns need. It's pretty easy. I listen to the radio a lot. Eat when I need to. Take a dump when I need to."

"Seems like a lonely job."

"It can be." He put down the food and braked as he approached a slow truck. The highway reduced to two lanes, taking away a safe pass. "Move it, jerk." The impeding truck moved to the right a bit, but Jerry still could not see around it. The truck slowed. "Move over, dipshit!" Jerry pushed on the horn heavily. Although he saw a hill, he decided to go anyway. Pulling completely in the oncoming lane, he revved up the engine.

A sports utility vehicle emerged in front of them. He sped up more, determined to get back over in front of the truck. The SUV moved to the right while honking as Jerry accelerated his small pickup.

"Shit," David whispered. He clutched the handle above his window as everything in his chest froze into a block of ice.

Jerry zipped back to his lane with seconds to spare. Hearing both trucks honk at him, he stuck one hand out the window and extended his finger. "Dipshits," he mumbled.

David, breathing heavily, clutched his chest, hoping to calm down his heartbeat. After a sigh provided more relief, David snapped. "Jerry, you may have been doing this a long time and used to pulling stunts like that. If you want to play with your life that's fine. But you're also playing with mine."

"What? It's their fault. The SUV or the truck should've pulled over or slowed down."

"There's no shoulder!"

Their argument was lost in a high-pitched sound. A glint flashed across the rear-view mirror. It happened again. The noise and flashes increased, as if gaining on them. The unassuming SUV had donned lights, and sirens. The flashing red lights inside the cab looked angry, and the flashing headlights played a game of "gotcha." Jerry cursed and slowly pulled over.

The window slid into the door, and he glanced at the highway patrolman. "License and registration, please."

He handed both to the patrolman. "You don't have anything better to do?"

The patrolman's head snapped up from examining the documents. "Sir, wait here while I check on something."

He rolled the window up to guard himself from the Texas heat. "I can't believe this guy."

"I can't believe you," mumbled David.

Both sat quiet, letting the air conditioning keep them cool. Eventually, the patrolman returned. "Sir, you've had two moving violations in the last 18 months. I'm citing you for reckless driving and improper lane change."

"What?" Jerry exclaimed. "I can't believe this crap."

"Sir, according to my radar, you were doing more than 20 over the limit. You made a lane change with a solid yellow line, and within a quarter mile of a hill. You endangered my life and the life of the driver in the pickup."

"I oughta throw this ticket away!" Jerry said while shaking it in the patrolman's face.

"I'd then have to cite you for littering. Drive safely, sir."

Jerry rolled the window back up while putting the ticket in his visor pocket. With the window cracked, he had to get in the last word. "Asshole."

David noticed that the setting sun not only cooled the air, but also Jerry's temper – until they reached Fort Worth. Jerry stayed in the passing lane, honking at anyone traveling too slowly and making abrupt lane changes. Almost to the office, he sailed through two red lights. He stopped when a car in front of him stopped for the traffic signal. As soon as the light turned green, Jerry honked. "Move it, dipshit. It's green."

Reaching the office, he took the documents inside and turned them into his boss. He showed David the proper techniques for checking the documents in and checking out for the day.

"So that's the life of a courier. Whaddya think?"

David stepped close and stared at Jerry angrily. "I may be new here, but you were downright reckless and unprofessional today. I'm willing to keep this between you and me this time, but if I ever hear of you acting like this again, or see it, I'll go straight to the offices about it."

***

Pushing the accelerator hard, Jerry passed the slow driver. "Jerk!" he said while honking. Still angry about David's tirade from yesterday, Jerry tried to imagine how he could have handled the situation better.

I should've told him I've been drivin' courier for ten years and he should keep his mouth shut, or I'll shut it for him. Or I could've told him to go to hell. Maybe I should've ...

His mind snapped to attention when seeing another slow-moving driver. Glancing at his speedometer, Jerry noticed he traveled nearly 90. *What is today? Everyone drive slow today?* "Dipshit!" he yelled while passing the car. Hearing a horn, he saw the car in the oncoming lane. Accelerating, he zipped back into his lane with a few seconds to spare.

A yawn deflated Jerry's ire. The sun started to drop in the western sky, taking away the gale force winds. For a split second, the beautiful orange glare took away his temper. The highway seemed lonelier today. He actually missed David in the car. Occasionally, he did train a new driver, which was something he enjoyed.

His stomach moaned. Jerry sped faster, wanting to get to a restaurant in the next town, then drop off the last bit of pharmaceuticals, then head home. The car seemed relieved when the engine stopped. Stretching his back and arms, Jerry tried to awaken his stiff, atrophied muscles. Popping his joints, he looked forward to a nice meal.

Sitting at his favorite booth, he did not even glance at the menu.

The familiar waitress appeared. Somewhere between fit and heavy, she had aged gray eyes that had plenty of wisdom—mostly from hearing stories. Her wrinkles disappeared in a smile, giving off a pleasant light. It was the typical small town café waitress who had the friendly ear and subtle wisdom. "Hi, Jerry. The usual?"

"Hey, Diane. Yeah – that'll be fine."

"How's the job?"

"Boring as ever. Picking up piss, drugs, and lab tests. At least all the idiot drivers make it interesting."

She smiled while filling out the ticket. "It'll be out soon, hon."

Jerry sighed, dreading the two hour drive back to Fort Worth. "Damn dipshit drivers."

"Not all idiots."

Jerry looked at the old man who sat in the booth next to him. Was he there before?

"They all can't be idiots," the old coot said. "To be honest, if you meet an asshole, you've met an asshole. If everyone you meet is an asshole, you're likely the asshole."

Jerry scoffed, glancing at the old man.

"Anger's no good," the old man continued. "It leads to prisons … and a terrible lot in life. Like the one I have."

The darkness almost hid the distinguished wrinkles and tired eyes. A red, faded ball cap had 'Stan's Trucking' stenciled on it. "I used to be on the giving end of anger, now I receive it … constantly."

Perplexed, Jerry wondered why a man who's voice had so much wisdom also dripped with sadness.

"When judgment comes, it comes back hard. It's made me lonely, tired, and I've learned my lesson a bit too late."

Jerry hunched his shoulders. "Learned what?"

"Ever since …" the man shook his head, unable to finish his sentence.

Jerry stood and glanced outside, noticing the large, black pickup. "That yours?" asked Jerry.

The old man nodded. "Yep. Been driving it for … years. I hope someday someone can take my place."

Jerry stood, wanting to get away from the bizarre old man. He rushed to the bathroom, washed his hands, then returned for dinner. "Good," Jerry mumbled, glad the old man had left.

The waitress finally returned with dinner. "So, Diane, what's with the old coot who was in that booth?"

She narrowed her eyelids. "Old man?"

"The one in that booth there," Jerry said, pointing at it.

Diane put her hands on her hips. "I haven't sat anyone in that booth tonight."

Jerry looked towards the other booth, wondering if he perceived the sitting arrangement correctly. No. A woman and her child sat there—and he remembered them. He pointed outside. "Remember, his cap said Stan's Trucking."

"Wait a minute," she said disdainfully, "the old man with the Stan's Trucking ball cap?"

Jerry nodded, finally taking a bite of his steak.

Her voice changed, with a mixture of eeriness and joviality. "Ooh, honey. You've seen a ghost."

"I don't believe in ghosts."

"Legend has it a guy named Stan disappeared on this highway about 20 years ago. His truck had this route to Abilene, but truck and driver disappeared. Nobody ever found him or his truck."

Jerry shook his head. "No way. The guy was here. Probably a new guy for Stan's Trucking."

"Well, if he was here," said Debbie, "he stiffed a check and my tip. And I didn't have to bus the table."

Jerry shook his head while finishing his meal.

***

A large semi sped by, spreading the dry Texas dirt behind it, along with the carbon monoxide. Jerry coughed. Wiggling his keys, he unlocked his small pickup, and got in. He sighed, grateful for the final delivery of the day. Finally, he could go home. Two more hours, then a weekend of rest and recreation awaited him. His wheels launched him onto the lonely, dark highway. Darkness spread in front of him, while the sun's light faded behind him.

Jerry's eyelids felt heavy. *Too much to eat*, he thought. He slapped himself and turned on the radio, trying to wake himself. After singing a few bars, he yawned, preventing any distinguishable lyrics. Quickly, he switched it over to a talk-radio station, hoping the host might stir some thought to stay awake. No. The eyelids tried to shut again. He jerked his head up and opened his eyes wide. As soon as he finished, they tried to closet again. He snapped his head to attention, hoping to stave off the sleep his body desperately craved.

The right side of his truck vibrated heavily, jarring him awake. Quickly he pulled off the rumble strip and back into the lane. Remembering a rest stop about 40 miles down the highway, he sped up to get there and take a short nap. Jerry's mind relaxed, shutting down.

Immediately his vision narrowed and blurred into darkness as his heavy eyelids shut.

A loud honking noise jolted Jerry awake. He pulled his head up and cursed loudly. "What the fuck?" Behind him, he saw a large vehicle with menacing lights. Too bright and too close, they almost blinded him. It honked again, sending an icy shot through his spine. "Back off, dipshit."

Another set of headlights barreled towards him as a monstrous vehicle blared a vicious howl. The terror almost seized him, but he broke free and turned back into his lane – barely missing charging semi. Jerry's car fishtailed, but he somehow steered and counter-steered enough to find control. Now his heart raced so fast and pounded so hard, it felt like a heavy weight on his chest.

Finding control of his terror, Jerry glanced at his speedometer, seeing his speed near 85. The vehicle behind him closed the gap. It was a large pickup, both in size and how high it was off the ground. Able to flip the rear-view mirror, he sped-up, trying to gain some distance. The truck behind him continued to remain close, as if taunting him. "I said," Jerry muttered while tapping the brakes, "...back-off."

The loud horn almost hurt his ears. It sounded three or four times – each one sounding angrier. The truck closed the gap again.

The loud honking started again, jarring Jerry's eardrums. He wanted to cover his ears, but he feared taking both hands off the steering wheel. Seeing the small shoulder, Jerry pulled to the right. He ignored the annoying vibrations from the shoulder grooves. "Okay," he said while slowing down, "…go ahead and get around me."

The vehicle also pulled over, maintaining a close distance to Jerry's bumper. "What the?" He glanced ahead, seeing nothing in the oncoming lane. "It's clear, you idiot. Get around me!"

The horn resounded again – bellowing louder as if releasing anger or sheer malevolence. Suddenly, an empty feeling tried to drag his chest down. Sensing harm as the driver's intent scared him. An ominous dread filled his chest.

Jerry moved to the empty oncoming lane, hoping the driver would pass him.

The truck followed every move. In fact, now it seemed as if the vehicle moved to make sure and get its bright lights into the side rear-view mirrors. "Damnit!" Jerry yelled. "What the hell is your problem?" He moved back to the correct lane, only to be followed again.

Defenseless, Jerry felt nervous and outmatched. He had a small delivery truck while the large vehicle behind him was a truck or SUV. The driver pulled alongside Jerry and flashed its lights at him. It honked again, startling him. He rolled down his window. "You fucking dipshit! Goddamned idiot! You're gonna kill …" An ominous dread filled his mind as his voice trailed into nothing. It was the same oversized black pickup from the diner. He noticed the license plate: EVL 666. Jerry might laugh but couldn't find any joviality to do it. Anger morphed into fear, and then hatred.

The truck swung to the left, then back to the right, dangerously close to Jerry's small pickup. He veered to the right while hitting his brakes. All tires left the pavement, and his small truck rolled across the plains. Tumbleweeds and tall grass slammed into his grill and thumped the hood. He crashed through a small wooden fence. Scared, he slowed more. A cow appeared in his lights. Veering hard to the right, Jerry barely missed it. Some trees appeared. Panicked, Jerry pushed the brake all the way to the floor. His truck jolted to a stop and his chest slapped the steering wheel while papers, pens, and trash all snapped forward. Dust rolled into his cab, trying to choke his throat and invade his eyes. Even though the air conditioner poured cold air on his face, sweat beaded down his forehead and made his palms slick. He quivered, actually fearing for his life.

Nearly 200 yards away, the black truck waited on the shoulder. Dust outlined its bright headlights. Jerry stared at the monster, forgetting his fear, and forging hatred. Furious, he grabbed his steel flashlight. Clutching it tightly, he imagined pounding the driver's head until it turned into a bloody pulp. "You Goddamned jerk!" he said while gaining anger with every step. "Get out of the truck!"

The horn sounded—slightly startling him. "I said get out of the truck!" he said while hitting the hood with his flashlight. The horn wailed again. "I said," Jerry yelled while reaching for the door, "...get out of …"

The door opened. Fiery eyes leapt at Jerry. The mouth, lined with disfigured, randomly sharpened teeth howled loudly. Cold, shadowy arms extended and tried to grab him. Jerry slammed the door and fell backwards. Panicked, he jumped up and rushed back to his vehicle. The shrill horn sounded again, leaving behind a cold, dreaded fright. In a full run he got back to his pickup, slammed the door shut and rolled up the window.

"You can't get away from him."

Jerry shined the light at the old man who was in the passenger seat. "What the? Who are you? What's going on?"

The old man looked as if he was about to cry. "I'm sorry. But he's lettin' me go and he needs a new driver."

"Get the hell out!" Jerry screamed while trying to push the old man out of his pickup.

More confused than scared, Jerry stopped trying to extract the man. "What are you talking about?   I thought you were …"

An invisible vice clamped on Jerry's neck. Feeling like cold steel, the touch robbed the warmth in his body. In his rear-view mirror, he saw it.   The monster's disfigured face looked as if it had been burned. Its eyes alternated between a hollow, black color and a fiery red anger. Its large mouth stretched wide, emanating a deadly hiss.

"So long, young fellow. You'll learn. Just as I did."

Jerry tried to reach for the old man's help. Ignored, he struggled against the powerful, cold grip. It clamped tighter. Soon, everything blurred…then went dark.

***

David stared at the long, forgotten highway while yawning. The road stretched endlessly, fading into a blur in the far distance. Soon, the sun started to recede behind him, trying to blind him in the mirrors. The empty miles obstructed his journey back to Fort Worth.

He wondered what happened to Jerry. He was last seen at a café several miles back – then he disappeared. The highway patrol could not find him, nor his truck.

David snapped awake as he approached a black pick-up truck. It traveled too slowly. Needing to get around it, David moved to the left. Unable to see very well, David lightly tapped his horn. The truck moved to the right then he zipped around it. "Move it, dummy!"

***

Jerry stared into the distance as the small pick-up got around him. He saw David. He wanted to beg him for help, but he couldn't. Tired, he wanted to sleep. Depressed, he wanted to cry. Hungry, he longed for food.   His passenger, though, enjoyed making him listen to everyone who passed him.

"Jerk!"

"Idiot!"

"You damn fool!"

"Get the hell out of the way!"

Every insult echoed perfectly in Jerry's ears.

BLIND NIGHTMARES

Roger felt too used to the dark. He barely needed a month for acclimation. Learning Braille, though, still had a way to go. He let Rex guide him to bed. Sitting on the mattress, he heard his dog curl into a ball on the floor. He smiled, petting his dog out of true gratitude.

Leaning back, his hands quickly found the alarm clock. By touch alone, he found the Braille signage and set the alarm. Reclining, he listened. He wondered if it would matter whether or not he closed his eyelids. Was it out of habit or ritual? Did he really need to close them?

At least he still had a job, and it was worthwhile. A dispatcher could still save lives, and over the last month, he talked a woman through CPR for her husband and directed another girl to save her choking brother with the Heimlich Maneuver.

He caught the scent of unlit candles. It was followed by the sound of displaced air. A new aroma reached his nostrils. "Sis?"

"How did you know?"

"I had a one in three chance," he smiled. "Besides, I can still smell your perfume."

"Good-night, Roger."

"Good-night, Sis."

Although subtle, the change was still abrupt. Light streamed. Images formed from memory. He could see again. Just like the previous night, they seemed faded, like a grainy photograph or a television that lost its brightness over the years. He heard it would fade to nothing within the next five to seven years.

The alarms sounded heavily. He rushed to the pole, dropped, put on his boots and threw on the coat. While getting in the truck, he put on the hard hat. The fire engine wailed while picking up speed. The urban sights quickly disappeared as they traversed down the highway. The captain addressed the crew. "We got a four-car collision. One vehicle on fire. Stay sharp."

Day suddenly became night. The lights became overkill. Every turn of the red, blue and yellow lights triggered a thump in his head. The headache grew worse. He tried blinking his eyes and shaking his head. Radio volumes grew louder, sounding faster, scared, and frantic. Voices meshed over each other becoming indiscernible. Road flares lit up the darkened highway.

The fire truck stopped, and the men scrambled.

"Paden," barked the captain, "you and Jones take that overturned car SUV."

More fire trucks and ambulances arrived – trying to confuse him. Used to such melees, Roger stayed focused. Underneath the black SUV, he heard a few people moan. Blood spilt on the highway, pooling with numerous auto fluids. The smell of alcohol was sickening.

Roger looked underneath the overturned vehicle. At least two moaned, while two others yelled for help. He quickly took control. "Calm down, we're going to get you all out. Just bear with us."

"Daddy!"

"What?" he asked the woman.

"Daddy!" She said it two or three more times – and then the voice and name registered.

He almost did not recognize her. Blood stained her face. Beads of safety glass were in her hair. Her voice, frantic, suddenly settled in his ears and into his heart, almost chilling it to a stop. "Candice?"

"Daddy," she reached for him then cringed heavily, almost crying.

His focus faded as his mind scrambled. Confused, he did not know what to do. His usual cavalier, confident attitude folded. Panicked – he reached for Candice's hand. "Don't worry," he said, "… I'm here, honey."

"Daddy … please. It hurts."

She's barely sixteen. She's not supposed to die. She's not supposed to be in a car wreck. She's not supposed … He shook the thoughts and tried to find the focus that eluded him.

"Get the hydraulic jacks," he begged. "Now!"

"Daddy, please help me. I'm stuck … and it really hurts."

Roger tried to pull the glass out of her hair and

relieve the pressure on her legs. Nothing budged. He struggled, hoping to jostle it a little and take away her pain.

A pump fell to the pavement. Another one fell several feet away. Roger yelled, "Get those things going!" The pumps started lifting the vehicle – and it took forever.

Another car caught fire. Firemen scrambled, begging for hoses.

Roger stayed with his daughter – waiting for the jacks to clear the vehicle off her legs. The other victims also limped like rag dolls, coughing, moaning, and crying. *Why don't those fucking kids wear their goddamned seatbelts?*

Roger pushed some broken glass and metal aside, then pulled Candice's leg straight. Carefully, he turned the girl next to her straight, and then the boy. *Three to get out? Shit.*

Feeling the heat, and hearing the frantic cries, he glanced at the bonfire behind him. One man turned the valve. The spray exploded. The clamp on the valve snapped like a bullet on the jack. The SUV collapsed again on Roger's head. He still heard Candice's dying scream.

He awakened, shaking. The terror of lost sight was pale to his pain of Candice's death. The still air carried the whisper of her name.

"You were saying Candice in your sleep, Roger. Did you have the dream again?"

Although he savored the waking blindness, the memories of his other senses kept a strong foothold in his mind. They kept the pain fresh, as if jabbing an open wound. The void of Candice's death grew, neither finding solace nor healing. "Yeah," he said quietly. "Thank God I can't see any more."

***

Jenna heard nothing but screams. They did not stop—but echoed painfully in her ears. Backed up against the wall, she wanted a place to hide. In darkness, she felt the wet, metal walls. Uneven, tiny, jagged points pricked her fingers. The cold, damp floor stole the feeling from the soles of her feet. "Mommy? Daddy?" She tried to use her voice, but it echoed too much in the contained cavern.

Something slimy crossed her neck. Jenna recoiled and tried to run, but her numb feet slipped on the cold, damp floor. All the wind left her body as cold water splattered on her face. Crying, she called out. "Mommy! Daddy!" She covered her ears as the noise reverberated painfully.

Getting up, she felt her way along the wall. The agonizing screams started again. Dissonant, the hairs in her ears jabbed her eardrums – almost making a painful hissing sound.

Something scraped her elbow. It felt cold, slithery, and wet. She screamed and jumped back into the corner. A feeble, wretched finger caressed her chin. "Stay away from me!" She flailed her arms as the cold, wrinkled finger returned, scraping her cheek. "Go away!" Her voice dissolved into sobs.

She wanted Busby. If her dog were here, he would protect her from the stalkers.

Jenna burst into a run, but after eight to ten strides, she slammed into another wall. She struggled to regain her breath.

Her toes felt the pain of sharp pricks accompanied with the cold, numb floor. A fowl stench reached her nostrils. The smell triggered her gag reflex and forced tears from her eyes. Manure? Rotting food? Unwashed people? The rancid odor nauseated her.

Jenna heard voices. They chilled the hairs in her ears. Some growls accompanied the whispers, sounding angry and hateful.

Something dripped on her shoulders. Thick, cold, she felt the liquid ooze down her arms, making strange paths to her hands and fingers. Suddenly, it burned – leaving blisters on her shoulders, arms, and back. "Mommy! Daddy!" she screamed, "help me, please!"

Jenna bolted awake, sobbing, screaming, and shaking. Sweat drenched every inch of her skin. She heard the light switch but remained in the dark.

She sensed two people rushing in and sitting on her bed. Catching the scent of Irish Spring Soap and Chantel perfume, she knew it was Mommy and Daddy.

"Honey," Daddy said, "what happened?"

Crying, Jenna felt his face. She felt the stubble on his chin. She reached for Mom's face, finding a softer face. "I had the dream again," she said between sobs.

Mom hugged her tightly, gently rocking Jenna. "It's alright, honey. We're here."

Jenna savored the warm, gentle touch, clinging to her mommy. She felt Busby jumping on the bed. The dog whimpered and snuggled close to her.

"Honey," said Daddy, "its okay. We all have nightmares."

She shook and trembled. Jenna spent her entire life in the dark and she was used to it … unless she had one of these dreams. "At least," she said between gasps, "when you have a nightmare you can turn on the light."

SLISH SLASH

Sallisaw, Indian Territory (Oklahoma) – 1856

Slish-slash, slish-slash, slish-slash, slish-slash.

Something moved behind Jonathan. "What was that?"

"Come-on, coward," said 12-year-old Joshua. "Nobody's out here." They stopped several yards from the burnt shack. "There it is: Black-Heart's house. She always eats the youngest." Jonathan peered inside the burnt shack. Joshua shoved him inside and held the door shut.

Jonathan covered his nose and mouth as a plethora of foul odors meshed into one putrid stench. A cold, rainy wind whipped through the cracked windows, rendering torn, tattered curtains into ghostly apparitions. Half a deer hung from a ceiling hook. It swayed back and forth, casting strange shadows. Dozens of candles lay scattered across the floor. Their flames struggled in the cold breeze. Dead, half-eaten rats lay in a corner.

He backed into a corner, catching sight of someone ... or rather some*thing*. It peered through a broken window. Frantic, he pounded the door. As he glanced back, the dark, gruesome figure scurried away. ***Slish-slash, slish-slash, slish-slash, slish-slash.***

Something moved behind Joshua. *What was that? A deer?* He squinted, trying to look deep into the thick trees. They hid something. Something dangerous. The door opened, almost knocking him off his feet. "Let's get out of here," said Jonathan, "something's after us."

He smirked at his little brother but lost breath as he saw the contents of the shack: the candles, the dead deer and the dead rats. Someone had been here ... recently.

"It's Sadie. She's after us."

Joshua shook his head, reminding his little brother the town folks burned Sadie's shack a month ago. He heard the stories of her violent screams. *It couldn't be her! The flames! The smoke! Being left for dead! How could she survive?* He tried to convince himself of Sadie's demise. Rational thought could not conquer his apprehension.

The rain poured heavier, almost angrily. Joshua buttoned the top of his coat and encouraged his brother to do the same. He readied his rifle and scanned the trees. "Let's get out of here." He feigned a smile while handing Jonathan a lantern. "Everything'll be all right. I won't let anything happen to you." He had trouble convincing himself.

Both boys moved quietly. They jerked their heads at the tiniest sounds. They flinched as high branches scraped their shoulders, backs, and necks.

Joshua remembered Sadie Blackheart. He had seen the gargantuan woman many times in town, mumbling to herself. People said she spoke magic spells that were used by witches and some Injun folks. Even the local tribes feared her. He knew some men burnt her home. They had bragged about hearing her dying screams. *Maybe it's not actually Sadie*, he thought, *but her ghost!*

The boys' fright subsided as they distanced themselves from the shack. Knowing the wagon was only another hundred yards away also calmed their fears. Both hoped to see it soon.

A grizzly, low-pitched howl rolled through the forest. It chilled the boys to a stop. Unable to tell where the sound came from, they darted their eyes in every direction. After a long, frightening silence, another howl rolled through the woods ... followed by a couple of whinnies and a crash. Joshua shot through the trees. Finding the road, he caught a glimpse of the horses in a wild gallop—dragging the wagon away. He burst into a run, yelling out "Whoa!" several times. He tried calling the horses by name – but they disappeared into the darkness. Falling on the muddy, rocky road, he bit his lower lip.

Where's Jonathan? Joshua looked frantically for his little brother. There he was. However, Jonathan's eyes widened, his knees wobbled, and the lantern shook. "What is it?"

Jonathan stammered and pointed. "Over there.

Look! See it?"

Something watched them. Its huge head bobbed. Some long claws, at least six inches long, raked down a tree. It scurried away. ***Slish-slash, slish-slash, slish-slash, slish-slash.***

"What was that?" Jonathan whispered while almost crying.

Shaking, his breaths in short pants, Joshua stuttered. "I don't know."

"A bear? A deer? A lion?"

"I said I don't know!" He tried to stop shaking and be strong. "Let's go. We'll stay on the road. I'll protect you. I won't let anything happen to you."

Neither talked. They moved quicker with every step as their visible breaths came out in short bursts. Joshua kept regretting his plan, knowing this was his fault. Part of him wanted to leave Jonathan behind so he could move faster. Loyalty and devotion ran deeper, though, and kept him from ditching little brother. He prayed to God, making all sorts of rash promises: not to fall asleep in church, to do chores without complaining, and to quit picking on his little brother.

Jonathan wanted to go home, crawl under the bed sheets, and pull the blanket over his head. He wanted to believe Joshua's promises, but he looked just as scared. He wanted Daddy. Daddy could stop whatever stalked them. He also wanted Mommy. Just hearing her voice would calm the dreadful feeling inside his stomach.

Slish-slash, slish-slash, slish-slash, slish-slash.
Jonathan stopped.   Joshua pulled his hand, encouraging him to keep walking.   The slish-slash sound passed to the right, deep in the maze of trees. Jonathan stopped again.   "Don't stop, dummy.   Keep moving!"

Slish-slash, slish-slash, slish-slash, slish-slash. Just barely in view, it passed just a few feet in front of them.   Joshua pulled the gun ready as his jaw dropped. Sadie Black-Heart!   Her legs had been burnt off, leaving only stumps.   She walked on her massive claw-like fingernails.   Her hair had been braided with bone fragments.   She smirked, then darted away as the long fingernails cut through the low brush.   *Slish-slash, slish-slash, slish-slash.*

They slammed their backs into a large tree, frantically looking around as their breaths raged out of control.   Joshua's gun kept changing aim every few seconds.   He accidentally hit the lantern out of Jonathan's hands.   Desperately wanting the light, he reached for it.   As he lifted the light, she emerged from the trees.   *Slish-slash, slish-slash, slish-slash, slish-slash.*

Resting on her stumps, she thrust her claws at Jonathan.   Joshua moved in front of his brother and aimed the gun.   She knocked the gun out of his hand then picked the older boy up by his neck.

Jonathan fell back and screamed. Sadie glanced at him then growled.   The old witch slashed at Joshua's mid-section once, twice, three times. His screams rolled through the forest as she laughed. She licked the blood off her face. Deciding to end his misery and take his soul, she sliced into his chest.

Jonathan's fear let go. He quit covering his ears, got up, and ran. He heard Joshua's body fall to the ground. Sadie chased him. The slish-slash sound followed as her long nails continued to slice the dead leaves and low brush. He ran faster, afraid to look back. Something jerked him back. His jacket caught on a branch. No! It was Sadie's claw. She drew him closer, swiping at him with the other claw. Frantically, he unbuttoned his jacket as she pulled him closer. His shaking hands had trouble grasping the wet buttons. He screamed as a swipe tore his pant-leg but missed the skin. After fumbling the last button a few times, he finally freed it, pulled out of his coat, and ran. Sadie got back on her nails and continued pursuit.

Finding an open field, he broke into a full run. However, the slish-slash sound kept pace. She reached for him in mid-stride, catching his pant-leg again. The fabric tore as he kept pace. She fell. He ran faster. The sounds of pursuit started again.

Something caught Jonathan's shirt! Lifted off the ground, he spun around on Sadie's claw. She howled at him, and the boy screamed. Maniacally, she laughed and reared her other hand back.

A bullet shot past her and detonated on a tree. On the main road, two cowboys sat atop their horses, taking shots at the monster they had seen emerge from the woods. Sadie growled at the cowboys, dropped Jonathan, lifted on her claws, and shot back into the woods. She quickly disappeared into the forest, blending with the trees and shadows.

The town created a posse to track her down. Everyone quit when they found Joshua, impaled on a dead tree. Written in blood above the body were the words:

Their blood will be on your hands.

The mayor wrote to the chief of police in Little Rock, and the governor, but both called the problem "hysterical superstition." The town council wrote to Washington, but President Buchanan called the situation "preposterous and absurd."

Of course, with any such legend, rumors tend to spread. The first is that Sadie bit off the heads of her victims. That was false. Her victims were always found impaled on dead trees.

Another inaccuracy was that Sadie only attacked white children. While she did prefer children, she attacked adults ... and Indian families as well. During the Civil War she killed 12 Union and Confederate soldiers one night. Surviving officers on both sides swore what attacked them was neither human nor animal.

One thing was for sure. Sadie had all the towns in Eastern Indian Territory (and some Western Arkansas towns) in her grip. Every town refused to let their children stay out past dusk—even on their own land.

Very few people survived. Those who did were traumatized with vicious, relentless nightmares. They always remembered the menacing slish-slash sound her claws made as they raked across the ground. Soon, she was no longer Sadie Black-Heart, but Slish-Slash.

***

Westville, Indian Territory - 1870

"Thank-you, Momma," Judy said, "I love you so much."

"A little girl should always be happy on her birthday—especially on her twelfth."

"Can I go now to get the ballerina doll?"

"You better wait 'til tomorrow. It gets dark quickly this time of year. We don't want Slish-Slash to getcha."

"I can be back before dark."
Momma shook her head. "No, child. Tomorrow. I know you. You'll get to talkin' to Becca and lose track of time."

Returning to her room, Judy paced. Knowing the doll was at Mr. Hall's store gnawed at her. She wanted it desperately. How could she wait until tomorrow when she had the money now? She tried to read a book from school. Distracted, it seemed like the doll called out to her. Unable to contain herself, she gently popped open the window. Easing herself outside, she moved behind the cabin towards the wooded area. She made it to the road. Scenarios played in her mind. What if

Momma or Daddy caught her?   Her little brother, Bobby, better not catch her or he would definitely squeal. Before long, she realized she only had a mile to town. She could get the doll and be back before anyone knew.

She moved faster—partly to avoid being caught, but more so to get her doll faster. It was a beautiful ballerina. She had seen it in the store many times. It was made in England, on the other side of the Atlantic Ocean. Momma and Poppa promised it to her many times. It would finally be hers. She could touch it and keep it in her room.   With high anticipation, the mile trek seemed short.

Reaching the store, she gave her birthday money to Mr. Hall. She smiled widely while finally hugging her new doll.

"Judy," said Rebecca, "you should see the new dolls my daddy got me."

"But I gotta go home and get back before dark."

Rebecca, though, assured her that looking at the dolls would only take a minute, and would have plenty of time to return home.

She was captivated at the craftsmanship of the Confederate Soldiers and the intricate design of the Southern Belle's. She listened intently to Rebecca as she explained who carved the dolls and the methods they used.

Stepping near the window, Judy froze in the setting sun. "Oh no! I gotta get home."

"So, you'll be a little late. Nothin' wrong with being late."

Judy put her shoes and jacket on then gathered her doll. "But it'll be dark soon, and Slish-Slash will be out."

Becca laughed, shaking her head. "You believe that old story? You're so gullible."

Shocked that her best friend didn't believe, Judy stood straighter, locking eyes with her. "You don't believe in Slish-Slash?"

"My daddy's been to the University of Chicago, and he says there ain't no such thing as a witch," she said smugly while crossing her arms and laughing. "Much less a witch with no legs that crawls around on long, sharp fingernails."

"What about them two boys she carved up near Sallisaw 15 years ago?"

"It was just one boy—and it wasn't no witch. Daddy said it was probably a mountain lion or bear that clawed that poor boy to death."

"I just know Slish-Slash is real," she said while shaking her head. "My Daddy's told me plenty of stories about her. Why would he lie to me?"

"It's just a story to frighten little kids. Nothin' more. Now quit believin' that stuff."

Judy did believe. The quandary played in her mind: rush home in the dark? Or confess and ask for a ride home? Realizing a whipping was in store for her, she confessed to Mr. Hall her disobedience. "I'm really sorry, but can you take me home in the horse and buggy?"

"Young lady, you made your own bed, now lie in it."

"But, but …"

"It's only a mile and I got work to do around the store."

"Daddy, she believes the old Slish-Slash story."

Unsympathetic, he shook his head. "Young lady, there is no witch, there has never been a witch, and I wish you children would not listen to your parents. Now you better get on home!" He did give her a lantern but insisted that she return it as soon as possible.

She pleaded with Mr. Hall to help her, but he would not listen. After arguing a few more minutes, he escorted her out the store and locked the door. "Face your fears!" he said while pulling down the shade.

She gasped. The setting sun frightened everyone inside. She only had one option: to get home as soon as possible. If she hurried, she could be home in 15 minutes. Surely Poppa would whip her—and Momma, too. Why did she come in the first place? Why couldn't she wait? Why did she stay to talk to Becca?

Keeping to the road, she moved quickly, not paying attention to the rocky and uneven path. She noticed the trees that surrounded her. They blocked the sun, rendering the road colder and darker. The naked trees seemed alive as the branches arched over, as if reaching for her. Worse, they served as a perfect shield for anyone ... or anything. Almost dark, a haze between red and orange peeked through the trees. A slight breeze rustled through, rattling the branches, and shaking more leaves loose from the twigs. It chilled her, forcing her to fasten the top buttons and pull her coat tighter.

She kept thinking about the Slish-Slash stories she heard most her life. True, no one in Westville had ever seen the witch, nor had she killed anyone from town in years. Maybe Mr. Hall was right. Perhaps they were stories to frighten children.

Judy, however, recalled a story from someone named Epperson who lived near Stillwell. He had seen Slish-Slash. Supposedly, she killed his hunting friend last winter. She also knew of an incident where three or four children from Tahlequah had been slashed to death by the old witch. On the other hand, they could be stories as well. She knew some false rumors about Slish-Slash had spread. But which stories were real and which ones were false?

She saw it! The monster reached out with long arms, a vicious terrible mouth opened wide, and the face with wrinkled and dried skin. Judy's chest wrenched on itself, freezing her breath, and locking it inside. She stumbled backwards, dropped the lantern and her doll. Looking at the ghastly witch, the light revealed an old tree. A large gaping, uneven hole resembled the mouth, while two smaller holes above it resembled the eyes. Two large branches spread out like long arms, looking as if they descended upon her. Judy's locked breath exited her chest, soothing her heart to a stop.

Picking up her doll and the lantern, she stood. Judy tried to shift her thoughts as she walked quicker through the path. Maybe a wagon might go by, and the coachman would offer her a ride home. No. Judy shifted her thoughts to her new doll, her 12th Birthday, and the dinner waiting for her back home. For a change, she felt a good tanning might serve her well.

Sounds distracted her. A woodpecker startled her. A few sticks underneath her feet snapped. An owl hooted. She stopped then looked intently into the woods, making sure nothing else looked under the veil of trees.

It seemed as if something watched her. Maybe she should go back to town. Mr. Culpepper lived closer. Maybe she should go to his house and stay there. Neither idea was appealing. Now, she was just as close to home as to town. Also, the Culpepper's lived atop a hill - and the only way was through the woods. She felt safer on the road. She continued to walk and tried to sing hymns - hoping that might alleviate her fear.

Slish-slash, slish-slash, slish-slash, slish-slash.

Judy lost a breath. She quivered. Her lower jaw shook. Her stomach dropped a couple of inches. Unsure if she heard the sound, she stopped and listened intently. The only sounds were some crickets and a few birds. The breeze died. She froze as the crickets stopped chirping. Wings fluttered quickly, giving haste flight to birds. She listened for any other sounds. After a minute of still silence, she heard someone breathing heavily. The breaths sounded painful, and hateful - like a rabid dog or wolf.

Slish-slash, slish-slash, slish-slash, slish-slash.

Slightly jumping, she identified the unmistakable sound. Scared, shaking, she walked. She moved faster. The sound returned. She exploded into a run. The sounds moved quicker, keeping pace with her strides. For a second, they were behind her. Then in front. They moved to one side, and then behind her again. The sounds stopped.

Judy stopped, frantically looking for the dreaded witch. Hearing the heavy breathing again, she took a few steps back. She bumped into something then froze as a hot breath poured down the back of her neck. An indescribable foul stench reached her nostrils. She wanted to run, but for some reason, remained still.

Finding some courage, she faced her tormentor, holding the lantern higher. Slish-Slash stood on her claws—which had a length of at least a foot. Her shoulders and arms had huge, powerful muscles. The witch scowled. Her eyelids narrowed and sloped downward, hiding her eyes. Sticks and pieces of bone dangled from her braided hair, clicking together. Her naked, charred chest huffed incessantly, pouring out the putrid, visible breaths on Judy.

At first the sight shocked Judy, but as she

continued to stare, the young girl felt sorry for Slish-Slash. She reached for her doll. "Would," Judy stuttered her words, "you like my doll?"

The witch looked at the offering. She dropped to her leg stumps, startling Judy – making her step backwards. Slish-Slash examined Judy, extending her hand, gently running her long fingernails through her hair.

Judy dropped the lantern. She cringed, closed her eyes, hunched her shoulders, and cried as the witch stroked her hair. Shaking, holding the doll, she prayed the witch might go away, or at least stop touching her hair. Slish-Slash withdrew her hand. Opening her eyes, Judy relaxed. Although scared, her breaths slowed, and she stopped crying. She desperately wanted to take a step and carefully walk away, but instead, kept still.

Slish Slash howled unexpectedly. Judy screamed and covered her ears. The old witch slashed the doll, tearing it into shreds. Judy bolted into a run. Slish-Slash picked herself up and pursued her. Judy cried as she ran. Her dress tried to trip her legs several times but somehow kept her balance. *Why didn't I listen to my mommy?"* The thought echoed endlessly. Her strides accelerated as the slish-slash sound moved closer.

Claws caught her dress! She fell! The witch dragged her closer. The young girl screamed, kicked, and grabbed for anything. Finding a large branch, she clasped it tightly. It connected to nothing! Judy was pulled closer to the witch.

Slish-Slash stood on the leg stumps, picked up Judy by the neck, and reared back the free claw. Judy screamed, closed her eyes, laid the branch vertical, and somehow blocked the blow. She thrust the stick and hit the witch's nose. Freed, she dropped to the ground and ran. Slish-Slash moaned, howled then pursued.

A few deer darted out on the road, scaring Judy. Able to dodge them, she continued running. A few of the animals screamed. The witch hit the ground. *Yes*! Judy thought, *slow her down*. The slish-slash sound started again. Realizing the stick was still in her hands, she tossed it over her head.

Slish-slash, slish-slash, slish-clump. The witch hit the ground hard then rolled several times to a stop.

Judy cut through the small section of woods between the road and her fields. She stopped for a second at the sight of her house and smiled. The slish-slash sound closed in–forcing her smile to fade. She burst into a run.

Jutting around the barn, she bolted to a stop at the menacing figure. Barely ducking underneath the witch's blow, she pulled the door open and knocked Slish-Slash down. Pulling the door back shut, she pulled the inside slat into the latches. The doors pushed inward under a force. Slish-Slash rammed them! Judy stepped back, watching the doors lurch at her. The young girl gasped as the slat cracked. She turned, moving past the sickles and other metal objects. They clicked together, casting strange shadows on the inner walls. The doors pushed inward again, almost fully breaking the slat.

Judy retreated to a stall and crawled under some hay. She peered through a knothole as the doors burst open. They emitted a long, painful moaning creak. Slish-Slash's menacing figure silhouetted against the moonlight. Fearful, Judy gasped, but kept quiet. Her lip quivered as the witch strode into the barn. She kept hoping Daddy or Momma might come outside. Surely, they heard her scream and the barn doors being rammed. Or maybe Bobby heard. Oh no! She would never forgive herself if Slish-Slash got Bobby.

A mouse scurried across her leg. She wanted to scream, but a paralyzing fear kept her quiet. Another mouse ran across her back, then a third. A few more followed, running away from the monster. Judy remained perfectly still and quiet.

Slish-Slash moved further into the barn, stopping at every stall. One horse neighed, while two others snorted as the monster scanned them. The witch moved deeper into the barn, ignoring the livestock. She looked around the barn, scanning high and low for her prey.

Wanting to make a break for the door, Judy crawled out of the hay as quietly as she could. Glancing back for a second, she could see Slish-Slash looking towards the upper loft. Judy scurried hurriedly, remaining quiet. Fully emerging from the hay, she brushed it off while standing and erupting into a fast walk.

Something caught her dress! Yanked backwards, Judy almost stumbled, but kept her balance while spinning. She bumped into the shadowy stature of Slish-Slash. The dank, warm breath made Judy almost throw up. Her heart froze. A biting cold fell through her chest, stomach, and then her limbs as she glared into the black eyes of the witch. Slish-Slash reared back her claws. The horses let out a bellowing neigh, drowning out Judy's screams.

***

One Year Later

Everyone trembled after learning of Judy's fate. A search party followed her blood trail from the barn to the dead tree where they found Judy's dead body. Judy's parents moved to Kansas, hoping the distance might heal their pain. Bobby took her death the hardest, never speaking a word for years.

Word spread about Mr. Hall's conversation with Judy, so people stopped shopping at his store. It closed, and he decided to move his family back to Chicago. He still insisted it was nothing more than a bear or mountain lion.

A few nights before moving, Rebecca took her doll collection to the tree where they found Judy's body. Near dusk, she laid all her dolls around the base of the tree then mumbled. "I'm sorry Judy."

"Becca."

She turned sharply. Becca cried softly at the sight of Judy standing amidst a rolling fog. Becca hugged Judy tightly, holding onto her as if her life depended on it. "Judy, I'm so sorry. I miss you so much." What was wrong? Judy did not hug her back. She remained stiff, and even cold.

"Becca, guess what."

Scared, nervous, Becca's body tensed. Muscles and limbs taut, she took a few steps back. Becca stuttered. "What? What is it, Judy?"

Judy smirked. "I have a new friend who wants to see your doll collection." Judy's face disappeared, mixing and fading with the fog. Becca saw an ugly shadow rushing towards her.

Slish-slash, slish-slash, slish-slash, slish-slash.

SLISH-SLASH V. YANKEES AND REBS

The gunshot echoed through the forested hills. Lifeless, the Confederate soldier's head dropped. Jake stared at the dead nemesis. Strangely, he felt nothing. Six weeks ago, after his first battle and virgin sight of blood, he spewed his guts and cried himself to sleep. Getting used to the carnage so fast worried him.

"Let's break this up," said the captain, "and get these damned rebels outa here." Angrily, the bearded commander pointed his gun at the other Confederate prisoners. "And let that be a lesson to all of ya! Any more actin' up or smartin' off, and you'll join him in hell!"

Jake's eyes casually shifted towards Captain Baxter. He found more hatred for the commanding officer rather than the enemy soldiers. Pulling the reins to the left and slightly squeezing his legs, the horse started its trot. He pulled alongside the wagon of prisoners. Six ... or rather five of the Confederates now ... headed north.

"Captain," said one prisoner, "how 'bout a funeral for our friend?"

Baxter pulled his horse alongside the wagon.

"Your 'friend' ain't nothin' more than a traitor to his country. I'll be damned to see him have a Christian funeral."

"You boys will be seein' 'im soon," said Lieutenant Richards as he lit another cigar. "Fort Berg will try you bastards and hang all of ya within a week."

"He was our friend. He deserves a decent burial," said the rebel.

Richards got closer, blowing cigar smoke into the enemy's face. "He's nothing but a goddamned traitor to the flag, to the country and President Lincoln!"

The rebel stared at the barrel of the gun, unable to hide his fear. "He ain't our President," he said in an angry whisper. "Jefferson Davis is our ..."

Richard's mouth scowled while holding his cigar. He slapped the confederate with the pistol then pulled back the flintlock. "Anyone who vows allegiance to *Mister* Davis, betrays the rightful, true President of this here United States."

Jake's breath froze. A lump got caught in his throat. Nervous, he shook. A strange mix of rage and fear slithered in his belly as he pulled him closer to confrontation with his commanding officers. "Sir," he said quietly, "let it go. He's no longer a threat to you, me, or President Lincoln."

"Stay out of this, Witt," Richards said coldly. Smoke from the cigar leaked from both sides of his partially opened mouth. The wagons stopped. Jake looked at Baxter, hoping the superior officer might step in. Unlikely. The captain was just as reprehensible. Baxter and Richards refused to take a guard off the chained men instead of fighting the attacking brigade. Too much battle and smoke disoriented the small nine-man cadre, and they ended up too far west.

"Sir," Jake had no idea why he pleaded for another life when it could jeopardize his good standing with his superior officers. "We're tired, hungry. Please. Let it go. He'll get his once we get to Fort Berg."

Gently putting down the flint, Richards never took his hateful eyes off the Confederate as more cigar smoke escaped his mouth. "Witt, just where the hell are we?"

Examining the maps vanquished his fear. After making a few calculations, then getting the position of the sun, Jake figured their location. "About fourteen miles into Indian Territory. There's a path near the Illinois River that'll take us right up into Kansas. We should make it there by noon tomorrow." He silently wondered if the Confederates would survive the trip under the draconian control of Baxter and Richards.

Finally relaxed, the group proceeded north. For a long time, the only noise was hoofbeats and the bouncing wagon. Weariness passed from Jake's body to his spirit. Wan, he sighed heavily two or three times, longing for two – maybe three days of sleep. Suddenly, his stomach growled. His mouth dried.

He took a sip from his canteen. The water left a thin coat inside his stomach, alleviating some of the discomfort. His hands reached into the saddlebags and found the beef jerky. Quickly, he ate some of the dry, old meat. Despite the bland taste, his belly felt relieved almost instantly.

A breath got caught in someone's throat. A bearded, pallid Confederate gazed intently at the beef jerky. The enemy soldier had a thick, red, unkempt beard. The over-sized clothes draped his gaunt body. However, striking Jake's heart was the look of hunger in the rebel's eyes. He glanced to make sure neither Richards nor Baxter noticed anything. He passed two pieces of beef jerky to the prisoner then let him sip the water.

"Thank-you," whispered the stranger. "I can tell you're a good man."

"I try to be," Jake said quietly.

"I could tell when you stood up for Carson. He's hot-headed. A bit too stubborn and full of hate. Thanks for not hatin' like some of those men."

"It's hard not to hate … sometimes. I've felt like them, but I fight that, too."

"This war's hard. It's like brother's fightin.' You got any brothers?"

Jake shook his head. "No. But I had a cousin the same age. We were like brothers. He moved to Georgia before the war to start a bank. Last I heard some Union Officers shot him on Sherman's March."

"Last I heard, my wife and little girl was burned to death in the March. At least that's what my Daddy told me in that letter. You got a wife and kid?"

Jake showed him the picture in his front pocket. The confederate looked at it intently – obviously amazed at the photograph technology. "That's my boy," said Jake. "Just turned 10. My wife died givin' birth to him. He's stayin' with my sister in Pennsylvania. I promised I'd be home for his birthday."

"I'm sorry," the confederate said quietly. "Name's Riley. Riley West."

"Jake Witt."

"Thanks for bein' a good man, Jake."

All the horses stopped abruptly and let out loud whinnies. They all stepped back, as if fearing the wooded trail. A few reared on their hind legs. Ears folded back, the horses kept bellowing, making shrill sounds. Charlie, the wagon driver, finally put down his whiskey bottle to keep his four-horse team under control.

The dogs joined. Their ears, too, folded back as they barked and growled. The ferocity changed to whimpers as their tails folded underneath. Just like the horses, they balked at entering the wooded trail.

Jake clenched his legs to stay on his stallion that reared on its hind legs. "Whoa!" he said. "Easy there, Nugget." As the horse put his front legs back down, he leaned forward and petted the horse's mane. "What's wrong, boy?" The horse let out a fearful neigh and stepped backwards. Jake caught the uneasiness of the animals. His eyes squinted, scanning the thick forests.

"Goddamnit," yelled Baxter, "I want these horses and dogs movin' forward!"

Barely able to hear him over the noises, Jared kept stroking Nugget's mane, hoping to calm his steed. Eventually, the animals quieted. Still, they seemed uneasy and frightened.

"Hey, Captain," said the lone Indian Confederate, "those woods are cursed. We must find another way."

"Shut-up, redskin," Baxter said disdainfully.

"But colonel, I tell you we will not survive the night. She will not let us."

Baxter pointed his pistol at the Indian. "One more word, redskin, and you'll be doin' your rain dances in hell."

The stoic eyes of the Indian filled with fear. His breaths shortened. Nervous, he shook as the gun barrel was set at his nose. "I am sorry, sir. Please. I was only trying to help."

Baxter removed his gun then whipped his horse with a riding cane.

"Captain, he's nuts," said Billy, the young corporal. "It's just some old legend about an Injun Witch. My grandpa told it to me when I was a kid."

Jake moved closer to Billy. "What's the story?"

"It's just a story to scare little kids."

And horses and dogs? Jake thought. He did not believe in ghosts. At least that is what he told himself. Still, he caught the uneasiness of the animals. His stomach churned and trepidation froze his joints.

Taking a deep breath and holding it, he hoped to stop his quivering.

Eventually, the horses continued – although Jake sensed the equines did so reluctantly. Every so often, they stopped and whinnied or neighed some more. His eyes darted back between the Indian, then at Billy. The Confederate appeared frightened, jumping at every little sound. He kept looking at the endless mazes of trees. He prayed in an unfamiliar tongue.

On the other hand, Billy smiled jovially, although he seemed frustrated over the balking horses.

Jake caught the Indian's mood. As the twilight sun seeped through the trees, the air slightly chilled. It added to his growing fear.

***

Moving to the prisoners, Jake and Billy gave them some turkey meat. Hungry, dirty hands clamored and took as much as they could. "We snuck some extra for you guys," they whispered quietly as he looked back at the jovial Yankees around the campfire. While his comrades enjoyed jesting and frivolity – and a slight inebriation, Jake did not share the festive mood. In fact, he kept scanning the darkened forest, feeling as if something watched them.

A couple of angry hands slapped away the food. "Don't want nothin' from you Yankee bastards," said Carson. Two other rebels shared hostility, spitting at Jake, the other at Billy.

Jake thought of slapping him—or perhaps clubbing

him with a gun. Finding some resolve, he stared at the dirtied meat. "Your choice."

"Sorry 'bout them," said Riley. "Hate's contagious. Like a disease."

"I think laughter's contagious," Billy said while smiling.

"If I had a gun, I'd shoot your traitor ass dead!" Carson said as he shoved Riley – causing him to drop the meat.

Jake shoved his gun in Carson's nose. "Listen up you asshole: I've gotten only four or five hours sleep over the last three days. I stood up for you back before we got into this forest. I didn't have to bring you any meat, but I did. Now if Baxter decides to shoot you, I'm not gonna stop him – I'll help him! As for Riley, he happens to be a friend of mine. You however, ain't," he said coldly.

Billy gently clasped Jake's hand, passing on some sort of tranquil, peaceful feeling. All the mounted tension ceased, helping Jake relax. He put away the pistol.

The fear returned. Taking it upon himself, he guarded the prisoners … and the camp. Clutching his rifle tightly, his eyes scanned the darkened, menacing woods. Naked branches crisscrossed making strange shadows that resembled demonic nightmares. The trees blotted out the light of the moon. A strange, tense feeling gnawed at his belly, which did not let him enjoy the warm, full meal. "Billy," he said quietly, "what was that story your grandpa told you?"

He laughed, shaking his head. "Just a silly story to scare kids."

"Don't you find it strange how the animals acted?"

"Probably smelled a Mountain Lion or Bear."

"Have you noticed," interjected Riley, "that since we got in these woods, we ain't heard one bird or owl?" He turned to the Indian. "Wolf, you said these woods were cursed. Watcha talkin' about?"

The Indian hesitated, as if hiding something. "I know nothing."

Billy stood while shaking his head. "You guys are just spooked. I'm going to guard the south end of the camp. And Jake," he whispered jovially, "if you here a slish-slash sound, then she's got ya."

Usually, Jake caught Billy's light-heartedness. This time, it eluded him. He stayed on watch. He talked for a while with Riley and exchanged family stories—finding an ironic friendship with the "enemy." They had much more in common than not.

Despite the friendship, Jake's anxiety never faded. A strange, unexplainable trepidation kept his eyes focused on the dark surrounding woods. Eventually, Riley grew weary and slept. Now, Jake remained the only one awake – except Billy. However, at the other end of the camp, he might as well be a mile.

Although he heard a few snores, they eventually silenced, giving way to the soft cricket chirps. Surrounded by darkness, feeling alone, he thought about his son. Usually, the thought of Daniel brought a smile to his face. For some reason, all he imagined was an orphaned boy.

He winced when the crickets suddenly stopped chirping. His fingers wrapped tightly around the gun barrel.

Slish-slash, slish-slash, slish-slash, slish-slash.

The strange, quiet whispering noise came from the northwest. Jake's eyes darted towards the direction, following the uneasy noise. He waited, hoping – and not hoping – that it might happen again. The dead, eerie air that settled around them seemed to block a refreshing, peaceful night wind.

Slish-slash, slish-slash, slish-slash, slish-slash.

The noise moved to the east. His ears perked. Definitely the same sound Billy warned him about. His chest tightened. He waited. Remembering what Daddy told him to do after a nightmare, he counted backwards from 100. As a boy, it worked all the time. Almost reaching ten, he realized it did not work now.

The noise emerged again, seeming to taunt him – trying to elicit a response. As it sounded a fourth time, it definitely seemed closer. Jake's lips quivered. His hands shook. He let go of his rifle, pulled the flint back on his pistol and put it the left shoulder holster. Slowly, quietly, he readied the second pistol, placing it in the other shoulder holster. He still felt no safer—even when he gripped the rifle.

As the noise sounded again, Jake quietly stood.

His breathing almost stopped as he took a gentle step backwards. Not wanting to make any noise, he moved stealthily, closer to the fire. All the while he kept his focus on the black woods in front of him. A deadly fear rendered his skin cold. Even when he stood next to the dwindling fire, the eerie silence chilled his spine.

Leaning on one knee, Jake clasped Baxter's shoulder and shook it. "Captain." Not waiting, he tried to jar his commanding officer awake. "Captain."

"Huh? What is it?"

"Something's out there." Jake repeated his words, keeping his eyes on the darkened trees. "Been circling us for about 10 minutes."

"Whadja hear, Jake?" asked Billy who squatted to one knee.

Jake did not want to answer, fearing rejection.

Baxter stood. "Are ya sure that redskin didn't spook ya? Maybe a bear, deer, or coyote?"

Jake shook his head. "No sir. Two legs only. I can tell. I want to take Wilson out to scout the area."

Baxter agreed and woke Wilson. The irritated private whispered a tirade of profanity while putting on his boots and retrieving his rifle. He carried the lantern in his left hand, while holding his rifle in the right hand. Jake kept both hands tight on his rifle, scanning left right, up and down in the light's perimeter.

They stepped in unison, keeping quiet—except for their quick breaths. A few times, Jake jumped as his weight crushed a twig. He worried the noise and light might give away their position. More concerning, he felt whatever waited for them had the advantage. Instinctively, he knew what stalked the camp was not human. Surely it had super-human strength, and it could see in the dark. Most monsters could. He kept hoping it was nothing more than a mountain lion or a bear. The hope drowned quickly amidst his apprehensive fear.

A fetid stench attacked Jake's nose. Almost able to taste the smell, his gag reflex tried to start. His eyes watered. He wished for a free hand to pinch his nose shut. He gulped hard to make sure nothing regurgitated.

Wilson suddenly stopped. "What the hell is that?" he whispered. They both moved towards the shadowy object. On the ground, it curled into a ball. Closer, Jake knelt and examined the animal. A ten-point buck, it had been cut open from the chest to the tail. "Deer," whispered Jake. "It's dried out so it's been here a while." Wilson pointed at another animal. Jake chilled, seeing the dead black bear. It, too, had been cut from chest to tail. The bear probably stood ten feet on its hind legs.

Wilson froze. His visible breath poured out his nostrils as his eyes widened. "I don't know 'bout you, but I get the feelin' we're bein' watched."

Nodding, Jake agreed. Part of him wanted to run. The other part wanted to find a hiding place. Earlier, he kept his fear in check. Now, it seemed too strong as terror seeped into his muscles and joints. A hollowed out feeling caved through his chest and stomach. His chilled skin moved on its own as the slish-slash sound emanated from the trees.

Surging to life, the trees moved towards them. As it moved, Jake saw it fully. It looked like a large, burnt woman. She had no legs, but only stumps. She scurried on her long, sharp fingernails that cut the dead leaves and brush. It made a slish-slash sound. Terrified, Jake froze. Wilson fired but missed. Jake lifted his rifle. The ugly woman dropped to her stumps then brought her claws in front of him—slicing the barrel of the gun. Shells fell across Jake's stomach, and he felt one claw nick his arm. He fell backwards. The monster shoved her left claw into Wilson's stomach then lifted him off the ground. The woman shrieked at Jake, then brought the left claw across Wilson's head. His blood splattered.

Jake's panic vanished, allowing him to spring to his feet and run. He almost tripped on another dead animal—and then a rock. Maintaining his balance, he bounced off trees and headed back to camp. Wilson's agonizing screams stopped. His lifeless body fell to the ground.

The slish-slash noise closed on Jake. It moved to the left of him. Then to the right. The noise stopped. At the perimeter of camp, he put on an extra burst of speed. The men already had their weapons drawn as he entered the camp. He tried to talk but it only came out as gibberish. He shook violently, trying to capture his thoughts. His breaths raged out of control. "My God, sir! It killed Wilson. It killed Wilson. It's after me. It's after me." He stopped his babbling and clenched his eyes tightly. Gulping hard, he fell to his knees.

"Calm down," Baxter said forcefully. "Just what is it?"

Finally able to seize the surging fright, he found his breath and frame of mind. "It's some sort of monster. Looked like a deformed woman of some sort." Catching sight of the Indian, Jake's anger swelled as he grabbed the confederate by the collar. "You! You goddamned redskin! What the hell is it?"

Jake finally noticed his Union comrades clutching his shoulders. The Indian sighed then remained quiet for a moment. "She is the Blackheart. You white men have a name for her: Slish-Slash."

A gentle hand rested on Jake's shoulder. "Come on, man. You don't believe this shit."

"Damnit, Billy," Jake retorted, "you heard the story yourself."

"It's just a legend. A silly campfire story my grandpa used to tell us."

"You, sir, have heard the stories," said the Indian. "I have seen her and her victims. She strikes at night, at men, women, and children. Those who survive have the nightmares."

"Just what the hell are we dealing with here?" Baxter asked.

"She is half Indian, half white. Shunned by both, she prayed to your devil and used our forbidden magic. A town tried to burn her home. She was inside and the fire burnt off her legs – but did not kill her. She stalks her prey on her long fingernails. These are her woods, and she will kill us all."

"You speak her language," said Jake, "can't you talk to her?"

"She will not listen."

Baxter stood, circling his stride to address his men. "Look, I don't believe this shit at all."

"Sir, please," pleaded Jake, "I know what I saw!"

"Witt," Baxter said forcefully, "you saw something – but it wasn't any monster. It's probably a rabid bear or somethin' like that. Am I right, Rains?"

"Yes, sir," said Billy

Baxter stood, barking his commands. "We're going out in a straight line, 20 feet apart until we find it. Charlie, you stay with the prisoners."

"Sir, we need to let them go and fight together."

Baxter grabbed Jake by his collar. "Are you insane? They're the goddamned enemy."

"We need every man we got to stop her …"

"I ain't fightin' with you Yankee bastards! I'd rather die! You're on your own against that witch!" yelled Carson.

Baxter fired a warning shot in the air. "It ain't no damned witch—and I'm not gonna lose any of my prisoners." He turned back to Jake. "Now git and find whatever it is that's out there!"

Still feeling his arms shake Jake clenched all his muscles. He thought the grisly site of war would have shielded him from such terror. Somehow, the monster dwarfed all he had experienced. She moved so fast from the dark. He vividly remembered Wilson being sliced through the chest. The dying screams etched perfectly in his mind. He remembered the strike of her long, sharp claws cutting through his rifle.

Sighing, he tried to exile the fear. Part of it subsided, but a heavy does lingered strong and loud. He lit a lamp and hooked it to the barrel of another shotgun. Moving stealthily with his team, jaw quivering, he jumped at every little sound. Surely, she would see their lamps and hear them. Having the night on her side, the witch could blend in with the trees and sit in wait for one of them to stumble on her. The fear subsided some more as he took more steps.

A grizzly, low-pitched howl echoed through the woods – chilling Jake to a stop. He whispered a curse as his insides churned heavily and shrunk to a heavy stone. The panic tried to return. Another fierce howl blared. Screams, whinnies, and yells followed. The wagon! The horses! The prisoners!

Bursting into a run, he rushed back to camp. As the men converged, they almost fired at each other but then shuddered still at the ghastly sight. All the horses and dogs had been cut and slashed. A few had legs cut off, and one horse had been decapitated. Most were still alive, emanating sickly, morbid sounds. The prisoners, all alive, screamed for help as the wagon teetered near a ravine. The four horse-team had broken away—but were cut up a few yards up the road.

Billy stood transfixed at the horror. "Holy shit."

Jake nudged him and the captain. "I told you it wasn't a bear! Do you see this? Could a bear do this?"

"I had to see it to believe it," whispered Billy.

"Get a hold of yourselves! That's an order! Now take care of these animals."

Jake cringed, finding Nugget alive. The horse looked at him like a desperate infant needing help. He had to close his eyes in order to put the horse out of its misery. More gunshots took the lives of horses and dogs.

Panicked yells alerted Jake. The wagon tried to slip off the poor road and into a ravine. He rushed to the wagon, jumped in, and tried to free the prisoners.

"Witt!" Baxter yelled. "What the hell are you doin'?"

He frantically looked for the keys. "Freeing them so they can get away!"

"I order you to stop it."

Although he imagined a gun pointed at his head, Jake ignored the rancid captain. "Damnit! Where's Charlie?" Feeling around the front of the wagon his hands and fingers tried to find the keys in the dark. Something felt funny. Hairy? No, it had skin. It was wet with something thick. Round. It felt like a nose, then a mouth. It rolled. Terrorized, he pictured Charlie's head and stumbled back. Something cold and metallic rested underneath his hands. The keys! The wagon slipped again. Jake rushed to the back and started unlocking the five Confederates.

"Witt!" yelled Baxter, "I swear to God, I will shoot you dead!"

The slish-slash sound echoed quickly. She emerged on the slope underneath Baxter. He turned and pointed his gun at her head. "You goddamned bitch!"

The witch fell from her claws to her leg stumps - dodging the bullet. With one swipe she severed the colonel's arm. Slish-Slash thrust her claws into his chest, ceasing his dying gasp.

Jake ducked as Baxter's arm flew close to his head. He fumbled the keys, finally getting Riley free from his chains. The wagon lurched off the road just as the two jumped to the ground.

Carson, yelling for his freedom, rushed the Yankee, Dobbs, and seized him by the neck. Pulling him closer, he let loose a tirade of profanities while strangling the soldier. Riley tried to call Carson's name, but the renegade soldier had gone berserk.

Jake tried calling Dobbs down then tried to separate the two. Long claws whisked by his head, severing Dobb's shoulder. She impaled him with her free hand. Slish-Slash reacted quickly, using her claw to catch Carson by his jacket. Leaning back, she drug him closer, then slashed his neck.

Breaking his frozen trance, Jake took his gun and clubbed her across the head. Unfazed, she pivoted at the waist and swiped her claws at his body. Jake turned his rifle sideways, blocking the blow. The other claw reached for his stomach! He closed his eyes, preparing for the painful stabbin.

A bullet hit her shoulder, knocking her back. Slish-Slash let loose her low bellow, curdling Jake's skin and hurting his ears. She lifted to her claws and scurried into the forest. Both Jake and Riley ordered a count-off. The men, too panicked, did not respond. "Get into a ring. Form a perimeter," said Jake.

The witch shot across the road. One soldier tried to shoot her, but missed, hitting another rebel. The Blackheart Witch impaled another soldier as her leg stumps hit the ground. Spinning, she hurled him off and sent him airborne into two other soldiers. She moved fast, getting on her claws then carving up the three men.

Terrified, Jake grabbed Riley and who fell next to him and bolted into a run. Two, maybe three sets of footsteps followed. The slish-slash sound rushed alongside, staying within the trees. They hurried faster, almost stumbling on loose rocks and uneven terrain. Jake wished he knew how many men were left. In all the confusion and her speed, he lost count. The slish-slash sound moved behind them—then to the other side of the forest. It sounded like she fell. Perhaps the gunshot weakened her. Unable to hear the slish-slash sound anymore, they slowed a little bit.

Spotting an old building, Jake pulled the others with him. They shot through a small graveyard, up to the porch then bolted into the doors. Huffing, they collapsed to the loose, weakened wooden floorboards. Dust kicked up into the air then tried to enter their lungs. They coughed, wheezed and grunted, trying to get their breaths back.

It seemed to take forever before they calmed down. Jake braced himself against the wall. His hands still shook. His jaw quivered. Finally comprehending the situation, he wondered if they would make it alive.

"Jake," Riley got closer with a candle. "You're bleedin'."

He noticed the vertical cut down his jacket and shirt. Feeling the blood ooze out, he grunted. The stinging sensation cut down his chest, stomach, and part of his thigh. Fortunately, the wound did not penetrate too deep.

Riley pulled the survival kit off Jake's shoulder. He warned Jake of a sting then poured the bottle of whiskey over the wound. Although he wanted to yell, Jake stifled his scream to not alert the witch. Riley then tried to help him off with the coat to apply some bandages.

"Get away from him you rebel!" whispered Richards. The Lieutenant pointed his gun at Riley's face, forced him over with the Indian Confederate then ordered Billy to seize their weapons. Billy hesitated but followed the command.

"Lieutenant," gasped Jake, "what are you doing?"

"I'm gonna have to shoot these traitors, Witt. Then I'm getting' you and Billy outa here."

"We gotta stick together," said Riley.

"Sir," Jake deftly felt for the knife near his boot, "listen to him. He's right."

"Sir," said Billy, "I agree."

"Shut up! They're traitors," he said quietly, yet forcefully. "Hurtin' this country. I gotta stop them."

"Sir," said the Indian, "please think about this. She does not care if we are Confederate or Union. She will try to destroy us all."

Richards spit at them. "You all burn in hell."

Jake stood and thrust his knife blade into Richard's throat. The cigar between his lips fell from his mouth as warm blood spilled on Jake's hands. He started to apologize to Richards – but stopped when he realized the regret would not be sincere. Richard's breath turned into a mere gurgle, then lost all life. Jake eased the dead body to the floor.

Billy and the two Confederates rushed to him. "Are we agreed to stick together?" Jake asked quietly as he pulled the knife out. They both nodded. He flinched, still feeling some pain.

"Injun—what's your name?"

"Was Hunting Wolf. Now—Running Wolf."

He wanted to take lead and formulate a plan. A

large clumping noise, however, forced all men quiet. The noise moved alongside the old, wooden church. A shadow fell over them as Slish-Slash strode by a window. The boards reverberated under her weight. The men scattered into the corners, hiding behind old, rotting, church pews. Jake peered from his hiding place.

The door swung open. The hinges moaned long and painful—as if wailing. She strutted across the floor, almost waddling as she shifted her weight from one arm to another. She swiveled her head while sniffing the air, perhaps trying to catch their scent.

Retreating, Jake hoped the witch would miss them. The loud clumps moved closer then stopped. She stood above him. His eyes closed as his breath froze. Unable to inhale or exhale, he clasped the knife—promising to slash her throat if she grabbed him. He kept praying she would leave.

A rat shrieked in the opposite corner. Slish-Slash moved towards the sound but did not do anything. She stared at the vermin, then at the old, decaying cross – only to turn her head sharply away from it. Slowly, she made her way towards the door. Stopping, Sadie Blackheart looked back one more time. She left.

The longest, tightest breath left Jake's lungs, providing the long-needed release from the tension that held him. He waited a few extra minutes, and hoped Riley, Wolf, and Billy would also remain quiet. A hand touched his shoulder, sending his heart into high gear.

He calmed, hearing Riley's voice. The others had joined him.

Jake took control. "Let's see how much ammo we got." Having a lantern, Running Wolf lit it. They laid out the small number of bullets they had found during the battle. Thirty-two—but half were for rifles. The only guns left were pistols. "Four bullets for each," said Jake. "We're gonna stay up on guard until daybreak," he said. "Hopefully, by then, she'll be gone."

They all retreated to opposite corners to watch the church. Earlier, all Jake could think about was getting away from the witch to save his own life. Now, he worried for the men he assumed command over. Often, his mind drifted to Daniel. He recalled Cathy's dying gasp when she gave birth to their son ten years ago. Both of their images, etched perfectly in his mind, were clearer than any photograph. The two events defined the greatest and worst day of his life. In the darkness, he determined Daniel would not lose his daddy.

Ironically, his eyelids became heavy. Weariness overpowered his fear, drawing him to the edge of sleep. Twice, he tried batting his eyes open and shaking his head, but the sleep his body longed for seemed too strong. His eyes closed.

"Billy." The whispers sounded soft and echoed a few times.

Jerking his head awake, Jake saw Billy moving towards the door. "Billy!" Jake whispered. The young soldier did not listen as if sleepwalking.

Suddenly, everything got cold. Jake's breath became visible and poured out his nose. Huffing, he crossed his arms, trying to find some warmth. The chill pierced his spirit. An eerie, menacing feeling froze his heart, his mind, and his being. The hairs in his ears stiffened. It felt as if cold needles pierced his skin. Jake stood to whisper at Billy again.

Stepping outside, a strange fog rolled across the ground. Rising up, the mist formed apparitions. They whispered for Billy, calling him by name. Fully taking form, they looked like Confederate Soldiers. Others followed. Children, adults, men, women, and some Union soldiers all moved in a choppy, uneven fashion. The visages did not walk but rather moved across the ground like something on a railroad track.

"I watched out for ya, Jake," said a voice. The image of Captain Baxter stood before him. "Ya disappointed me, son."

"Billy," said Jake as he pulled back the flintlock, "don't listen to them. They're not really here."

Suddenly, Running Wolf and Riley joined them. They, too, seemed bewildered by the multiplying guests. While a few looked like their former comrades, many consisted of children, men, women, Indian, white, and black. Who were they? Victims? They kept calling Billy, then for Riley, and even Running Wolf. All three were stuck in a trance.

They did not listen to Jake. His mind panicked,

wondering how to save them. How could he do this alone? Or could he escape without any help? Jake fired his gun into the air.

The ghosts disappeared. The men woke up.

A large, iron-like grip clasped around Jake's neck. Her claws hovered around his head like a murder of crows. While hissing, Slish-Slash lifted him off the ground, straining his neck. He kicked, trying to find balance. It only worsened his plight. He tried to thrust his knife at her, but she caught the arm with her other hand. She pulled it tightly then squeezed hard. His knife fell to the ground. He kept trying to inhale but could not find any air. Worse, it felt like she was about to pull his arm out of its socket.

A gun pointed at Sadie Blackheart's head. "Let him go," Riley said forcefully.

A second gun aimed at her head. "Right now," said Running Wolf.

Billy pointed a third gun at her head, giving Slish-Slash no other options. She gazed at each one of them then gently lowered Jake to the ground. He coughed, finally finding the air his lungs craved. Holding his throat, he tried to alleviate the heavy pain in his throbbing neck.

Getting his breath back, he glared at the witch who faced the three guns. She did not seem so menacing now. In fact, on her leg stumps she barely stood five and-a-half feet tall. On the claws, though, she'd be over six feet in height. Her shoulders and arms had huge muscles. Somehow, the hatred in her eyes could be seen in the dark. They tried to hide behind her large forehead. She had a large, sharp nose. Definitely intimidating were the pieces of bone she used to braid her hair.

Her loud bellow rang through the air as her arm whisked fast across the three men. Their guns discharged but were knocked out of the way and out of their hands. Not one bullet hit her. Slish Slash stared at her prey. They all huffed but did not move.

Slish-Slash used her claws to snag Billy and Riley by their coats. She looked them over, paying close attention to their faces – and then their uniforms. After gawking at them for a few minutes, she released them. However, her quick claw caught Running Wolf and dragged him closer. He prayed in his native language, while she examined him for a long time.

She released him, then caught Jake by the coat and pulled him closer. He wanted to pinch his nose shut from her awful stench. Moreover, her putrid, visible breath poured over his body. Her crooked, and jagged teeth looked ready to bite his head off. She took a long look at his uniform then poked at his medals with her free claw. Finally, her eyes met his. Black, hateful, they cut through his soul. As the evil emanated, it tried to slither its way into his heart. Despair, terror, and dread poisoned his soul, trying to drag him into a black abyss. He closed his eyes as his breath stuttered. Silently, he prayed, but soon it came through as audible whispers. "Please. I got a boy."

Her nails released Jake. The men jumped back as she lifted to her claws. Slish-Slash lumbered into the woods, shifting her weight from one shoulder to the other as the long fingernails hit the ground. *Slish-slash, slish-slash, slish-slash, slish-slash.* Soon, she disappeared and the noise faded.

***

Jake opened his eyes abruptly. His jaw quivered.

"Pa?" said Daniel as he opened the door, "are you all right? Sounded like you had another nightmare."

Jake sat up, lighting a lantern. He glanced at the letter he got yesterday. He read it for the tenth time, transfixed on every word:

> *Dear Jake,*
>
> *Billy and Wolf and I really enjoy it here in Ohio. Our blacksmith shop is doing well. Billy's falling in love, and I have a right pretty woman, too. Despite the nightmares, we don't tell our women about that night we survived. We usually end up telling them how sad we are that this country's still hating each other – even though the war's been over for six months.*
>
> *I've looked through some old newspapers and finding more reports of Yankee and Confederate Soldiers missing near Arkansas and Indian*

Territory. My guess is that she got at least 40 people. I cannot figure out for the life of me why she spared us. Maybe it was because we didn't hate each other.

You're my good friend and my brother. I miss you -- and maybe we'll see each other around Christmas.

Your friend, Riley West

Daniel walked closer, looking afraid. "Pa," he said quietly, "you okay?"

Jake flinched. Slish-Slash gazed through the window at Jake and Daniel. Everything inside his chest stopped as she waved at them with her claw. Closing his eyes, Jake took a deep breath. She disappeared.

"Watcha lookin' at, Pa?"

Jake feigned a smile. "Nothing, son." Clutching his son, Jake looked at him. "Daniel, I've told you not to hate anyone, haven't I?"

"Sure. All the time."

Finding a real smile, Jake nodded. "Good. Don't you ever forget that."

THE BALLAD OF SADIE BLACKHEART

On her hands and nails she stalks her prey
Taking children, the innocent lambs
And men, and women, lives and souls
Her hatred is for all those in the land

One night the Blackheart conjured spells
In her tiny one-room shack
With their torches the townsfolk burned her home
"Go to hell, Sadie! And don't come back"

Her hate and spite stayed alive
As her legs burned into the ground
Crawling on her nail-like blades
It's her if you hear the "slish-slash" sound

She slices, she stabs, she strikes them all
With her long knife-like nails
After stalking frightened traveling souls
Who walked those darkened trails

So, in the woods, late at night
Away from sacred ground
Be sure to be right with your Maker
If you hear that slish-slash sound

THE NIGHT THE DEVIL CALLED A
CHRISTIAN RADIO TALK-SHOW

Pheonix, AZ – 1996

Jack hit the flashing button. "Hello," he spouted off quickly. "You're on Conversations with Jack McKay."

"Am I really on the radio?"

Although the woman could not see, Jack still smiled and nodded. "You sure are. What do you want to talk about."

She drew out a long "well" before continuing. "I wanted you to know I listen to you every day and I really feel blessed when I do."

"Thank you. And I'm talking to ... ?"

"Cherri," she said quickly. "And I want to know what can I do to help?"

Jack scratched his light-brown, well-shaven beard. "Well, you can always make a tax-deductible donation." He glanced down at the other blinking phone lines, realizing others were waiting. He needed to end the conversation. "And you can always pray for the people I try to minister to."

"Okay," said Cherri. "Thanks again, Jack."

He started to hit the kill button.

"Oh Jack ..."

He stopped and looked at the phone line, superimposing the vague picture he had of Cherri. "Yeah, Cherri?"

"God bless you."

He smiled, returned the blessing, then went to the next phone call. "Hello, you're on the air with Jack."

"Yeah," the male voice stammered, sounding scared. "Um ... I want you to know that I'm gay and I don't think ..."

"You're a homosexual?"

"Yeah. And I don't think a good God will send me or anyone else to hell just because ..."

Jack's anger flared up at the young man's disrespect and poor concept of Scripture. "Well, what you think and what's the truth are two entirely different things. Don't you know that God classifies your sins with those of incest and bestiality?"

"Well ..."

Jack yelled back. "Answer me!"

"Shut up!" the listener fired back. "I was talking."

Jack lowered his tone. "But this is my show." Noticing Kevin give a thumbs up, Jack returned the sign to his call screener. He went back to the listener who was spouting off studies showing homosexual tendencies to be rooted in genetics. "Look ...." Jack tried to remember his name. "What's your name?"

"Darren."

Jack immediately went into his speech about the

homosexual agenda. He spouted off statistics of sexually transmitted diseases among homosexuals and their projected number of partners. As Jack started to quote the Scripture of Romans 1, Darren yelled back. "Listen to me!"

"I don't have to listen to you," said Jack. "You are an abomination to the Lord. You are full of sin and corruption. And I'm going to pray for you."

Darren's voice, full of mistrust and anger, spilled viciously through Jack's earphones, almost distorting. "Don't pray for me!"

"I am," said Jack as he closed his eyes. "Father I pray for Darren ..." Jack's prayer continued despite Darren's protests. When Jack finished with an "amen," he heard Darren swear at him. Frightened at the thought of protests or complaints, Jack hit the kill switch.

The next caller was a confessed "liberal" woman who thought Jack's views on abortion and contraception were barbaric. Losing control of the caller, Jack put her on hold, then looked over at Kevin who simply hunched his shoulders. After sighing, Jack thought he could talk to her again. Cupping his palms over his mouth, Jack inhaled deeply, closed his eyes and let her back on the air. They argued for a few minutes, then Jack finally let loose his cannons. "It's your fault that America is declining. Your lost, inept values have influenced our public schools and have taken us down a road of irresponsibility and anarchy. Hell is waiting for you."

"I don't believe in hell!"

Jack cut her off. His next conversation was a Satanist who again got into a shouting match with Jack. This fellow, who refused to identify himself, said he had several tattoos and body pierces, and that he listened to black metal music. He tried to convince Jack that Satanists do not commit human sacrifices. Jack shook his head, then yelled at the Satanist. The radio jockey then offered a prayer to the listener. The caller did not listen. Jack finished his prayer, then disconnected the caller.

Jack sat back in the chair triumphantly. Putting his feet on the panel, he locked his fingers and cradled his head in his hands. His smile quickly evolved into a prideful laughter.

"That was great, Jack," yelled Kevin who started the string of commercials.

Jack leaned forward on the counter and cast an angry glare at the intern. "Kevin!"

The young intern yanked the long bangs out of his eyes and crossed his arms. He looked like a defiant child of the 1970's: the faded jeans, the drab green shirt, the glasses and the goatee beard. Kevin leaned against his control panel. "What, Jack?"

"Screen those callers better. I can't have people swearing on the air! If the FCC doesn't shut me down, the people of Phoenix will."

Kevin shook his head. "Just be cool about it. It's not the end of the world."

"It's not your radio show," Jack said while loosening his tie.

"You got five seconds," Kevin said while shaking his head. "And you're going to love this next caller."

Jack put his headphones on, listened to the feed, then gave his usual, brief introduction. "Here I am, Phoenix. Like it or not, the truth is here in my profound words of wisdom. All rooted in the Bible, all rooted in the Gospel ... and all rooted in Christ." He punched the button. "You're on the air with Jack McKay."

"I wanted to call," the caller said in a soft, low voice, "... to say I love your show." The voice emanated a slight echo that resonated deeply.

Jack examined the control board, trying to find a cause for the glitch. "Well," Jack said as he looked for the problem, "...thanks. And you are?"

"Oh, come one, Jack. We were friends once."

Jack tilted his head, trying to recapture the ominous, yet familiar voice.

"You chased me for many years," the caller said. "And now, you help me more than you know." The voice got lower, seeming to stay in the caller's voice box or throat.

Jack tried to remember the voice, but it eluded him. "Come on. Who is this?"

"The Devil."

Jack's laughter started silently but then bellowed loudly through the control room. Soon, Kevin's laughter mixed in and both radio men spun around in their chairs. "So, you're the Devil. Satan. Lucifer. Father of Lies ..."

"Don't treat me with contempt!" The voice startled Jack. Leaning back in his chair, he felt a slight chill. Tension churned in his stomach and swelled into his chest.

"I know all about your college days," the caller said. "The parties, the drinking, cheating on exams ..."

Jack noticed his fingers shaking. He clenched a fist as he spoke into the microphone. "I've told my testimony many times on the air. Who is this?"

"You don't believe me?"

Jack's heart slowed dramatically, although his breathing increased. Kevin still smiled, letting out muffled laughs, but Jack felt weird. "No ... no I don't," he said while shaking his head. "I ... I ... I mean ... wh ... why ... why would ... the devil ... call ... me?"

"Do you want proof?"

Jack shook his head, then remembered the caller could not see him.

"You don't want proof?" the caller asked.

Taken aback, Jack did not know how to respond. How did he know I shook my head? Nervous, Jack looked around for any clues. Chill, Jack, he had a 50/50 chance. Gaining back his confidence, Jack raised his voice slightly. "I don't need proof. The devil is a phony. And so are you. This joke's gone too far. Goodbye!" Jack cut off the listener, then glanced at Kevin.

Kevin held his arms out, shook his head, then hunched his shoulders.

Jack hit the next line. "You're on the air with Jack McKay."

"That was awfully rude."

Jack narrowed his eyelids as the foreboding voice echoed again over his earphones.

"What's the matter, Jack? Cat got your tongue."

Jack looked at the grid. Yeah, he cut off the person. Multiple phone lines? he thought.

"Jack, this guy's obviously a psycho," said Kevin over the secret line that did not go over the air. "Keep him on and calm him down and I'll call the police to trace the call."

Kevin grabbed the phone and dialed for the operator.

Jack relaxed in his chair, then yanked the tie off. "If you're really the devil, then why call a Christian radio talk-show?"

"Don't you want an exclusive?"

The fright returned. Jack's muscles tensed, and he felt an overwhelming sense of fear. Calm down, Jack. If it is the devil, he has no power over you. Yeah! Try that. Jack smiled. "If you really are the devil ... then go away in the name of Jesus."

The caller laughed hideously. "Jesus, I know. But who are you?"

Jack's lower lip quivered at the laugh. He tightened his jaw, gulped, then wiped the sweat off his large forehead. "You're supposed to submit to the name of Jesus."

"You play with the name of Jesus, like those stupid, inane Sons of Sceva. You wield that holy name around like a child playing with his father's lighter. You believe in Jesus? Well remember, so do I ... and I tremble."

Jack felt some anger boil and explode. "Hey! I'm a Christian. Washed in the blood of the Lamb. The Holy Lamb of God! You must obey me!"

The voice grumbled lowly. "Jesus I will submit to, "the voice exploded, " ... but never to YOU!"

Jack yanked off the earphones and covered his ringing ears. Kevin, too, held his ears. Composing himself, Jack put the earphones back on.

"Better?" asked the caller.

Jack nodded.

"Good."

Jack glanced over at Kevin. I'll bet people are tuning in now. "Devil, " Jack could not believe what he was saying, "...why call me? Why thank me?"

"Because you help me."

"I help you?"

"More than you ever know."

The line shut down, now only filled with static. Jack sat there for a minute, silent. His mind raced for any plausible, logical explanation. Ham radio operator? Multiple lines? Bugging devices? A prank call?

Kevin pounded on the studio window and waved at

Jack. The jockey jumped out of his trance and looked at the calls. Frightened, he hesitated, then looked at the clock. He inserted a feed to introduce the next jockey. "It's uh ... it's uh ... now 7:55 p.m., and ... it's uh ... time to shut down Conversations. Stay tuned for the No Alternative show with Charlie Kyle. This is Jack McKay, signing off and reminding you I will be back tomorrow from 6 to 8 p.m. right here on your KSTN, 101.7 on your FM dial."

Jack hit a button and let the lead play then rushed to the outside booth. "Did they trace it?"

Kevin, on the phone, looked up at Jack and shook his head. "Weren't on long enough." After hanging up the phone, Kevin leaned back in the chair, almost laughing. "Boy what a weirdo."

Jack shook his head. "Not funny, Kev."

Charlie marched in, smiling widely as he carried some compact discs.

"Charlie," Kevin said as he spun his chair around. "Did you get a load of the last caller?"

Charlie stopped, pulled his hair back and fasted it into a ponytail. Although many hairs had turned gray, his thin face and childlike eyes made him seem much younger than he really was. "What last caller?"

"The caller who said he was the devil."

Charlie laughed as he arranged the discs near the players. "Didn't hear it," he said, shaking his head. "On my way up, it was dead air. Probably for two, maybe three minutes. All I could think was that the people of

Phoenix were safe from Jack McKay."

Jack moved to the restroom. His mind wandered to how someone could have pulled off such a prank. Maybe Kevin was in on something. Something passed behind Jack. Shadows seemed to move, darting around, barely escaping his view. Startled, Jack turned, then jumped back at the sight of his own reflection. The nervousness returned, along with the fear. Sweat drenched his palms, his muscles tensed, and his stomach tied into knots. The door pounded loudly, scaring Jack again.

"Jack! Jack!"

Embarrassed, Jack composed himself and opened the door. Kevin stood in the doorway. The young intern's eyes were wide, displaying a skeptical disbelief. However, a large casual smile spread across Kevin's face, confusing Jack all the more. "Listen to this," said Kevin as he led Jack back to the control room. "I was listening to the reels of the last caller to get an idea of who he was and to make sure we broadcast."

Jack hunched his shoulders. "So."

"Listen." Kevin played the conversation. However, the derelict, ominous voice was missing. Kevin laughed as he watched Jack's mouth drop open. The intern smiled, made some eerie noises, trying to imitate a ghost.

"What are you two doin'?"

Jack and Kevin jumped, then looked at Charlie who poured some coffee.

"That last caller really spooked him," said Kevin.

"Said he was the devil," added Jack.

Charlie laughed, letting his whole face lighten.

"Why would the devil call a Christian talk-show and thank me?" Jack asked.

"Oh, come on," Charlie said while smiling. "If it was the devil, of course he's thanking you."

Jack put his hands on his hips. "Oh, come on yourself. Let's get real here. Why would he thank me?"

Charlie kept smiling as he shook his head. "You are really so full of pride you can't see it can you?"

Feeling defensive, Jack leaned against the counter, then swelled his chest. "See what?" he asked defiantly.

Charlie took a sip of the coffee, then set it down. "I've listened to you enough to know that you alienate people."

"I'm spreading the Gospel!"

Charlie shook his head. "No, you're not. You're on some sort of crusade or inquisition ..."

"Wait," said Kevin, "...it's unfair to qualify Jack as a crusader because he hasn't killed anyone in the name of Jesus. At least not yet."

Charlie, leaning on the doorframe and finally, stopped smiling. "But it's the same attitude. You may not be killing and maiming in the name of God, but emotionally and mentally, you're destroying those you're trying to reach."

Jack protested loudly. "We're on the same team, man!"

Charlie finally let some anger flare up in his eyes – as well as his words. "I agree with some of what you say, but it's how you say it that bothers me. We may be on the same team, but it seems every time Christians make a long-distance run, it's called back for your holding penalty." Charlie moved closer. "Do you know what you do with every caller?"

Jack, feeling a loss in the attack, resigned to silence.

Charlie counted on his fingers. "One, you don't listen. Two, you throw their sins back in their face. And three, you don't offer forgiveness. If you led with grace instead of judgment, you might see more fruit for your ministry, more respect and less hate-mail." The older disc jockey shook his head. "But then, that wouldn't get you ratings. Right?"

Feeling deflated after a very successful show, Jack draped his jacket over his arm and left the studio.

***

Jack turned over again, trying to get comfortable. He flipped the pillow to the cooler side, then lay on his stomach. Charlie's words kept replaying in his ear, preventing sleep. Maybe I should try it like he said. Able to close his eyes, he relaxed.

Jack jarred awake as the phone rang.

Using a neutral curse word, Jack hoped whoever called him at this hour had a good reason. He activated the cordless phone. "Hello? Who is this?"

"Don't listen to Charlie!"

The dark, ominous, and familiar voice sent chills down Jack's spine. He shut off the phone then scanned the darkened room. Shadows took on horrific shapes, then stealthily moved through the room. They whispered something, but the volume was too low and the words indecipherable.

The phone beeped again. Jack answered angrily. "Leave me alone! I'll have this call traced and call the police!"

"If you take Charlie's advice. You'll lose everything!"

Jack killed the connection, hoping it would do the same to the caller. The phone sounded again. He got out of bed. Something inside him wanted to answer its beckoning, but scared, he backed away from it to remove the temptation. Unable to contain himself any longer, he reached for the phone, but it stopped.

The shadows stopped scurrying up, down, and across the walls and ceiling, returning back to their original, harmless forms. However, Jack felt as if strange sets of eyes watched him, waiting patiently for him to make a mistake. He grabbed a golf club and moved stealthily through the dark, keeping his back to the wall. The shadows returned to life again, circling him ominously. They seemed to grow arms that reached for him. His breaths came in short pants and his stomach tied into knots.

I gotta get out of here! He darted towards the living room but stopped as a when the ghastly fear turned into a quiet stillness. Jack dropped the club, then glanced back at a shadow. It stood high and wide, forming a perfect cross. It hovered over his kitchen table, as if guarding his home. All fear vanished as he stared at the shape, and even more so as he heard a quiet, subtle voice. "Well done good and faithful servant. Well done."

Jack smiled, closed his eyes and sighed. "Thank you," he mumbled as he left the kitchen and went back to bed.

Headlights moved across the kitchen wall, changing the outline of the shadow into a hideous creature. Its wings spread out like a large bat, and its head grew grotesque ears that resembled those of a hyena. Red eyes glowed amidst the shape, and an evil smile spread across its head.

***

Jack opened the envelope. The figures on the check wowed him. Excitement brewed. A letter from the station manager congratulated him on the latest ratings - which were number one for the timeslot. He recalled the words he heard last night, "Well done good and faithful servant. Well done." Excited, he punched the air victoriously.

"If you're through congratulating yourself, then take this next caller when the commercial's over," Kevin said over the intercom.

Jack gave Kevin a thumbs-up and smiled widely and hit the line button. "You're on Conversations with

Jack McKay."

"This is Darren again."

Jack thought for a moment. "Oh," his eyes lit up, recalling the conversation, "...the perverted homosexual I prayed for. Have you repented yet and accepted Christ as your personal savior yet?"

The voice, weak and distraught, sounded defeated. "No. I'm afraid ..."

Jack cut him off sharply. "You're afraid of the Cross of Christ? Or maybe you're afraid of the fires of hell? Or are you afraid that one day you'll die of AIDS? Or perhaps shot by a jealous gay lover?"

Jack yanked his earphones off and jumped back at the gunshot. The noise resonated, causing Jack's ears to ring. Frightened, he put his mouth close to the microphone and called out to the boy. "Darren?" Nothing. "Darren are you still there?" Jack's stomach tightened, then churned. He yelled louder. "Darren ... talk to me ... please."

"I'll call 911 and get the get the operator to trace the call," Kevin said over the intercom.

Jack took a deep breath, hesitated, then moved closer to the microphone. "I'm sure all of you are shocked just as much as I was by Darren's suicide. You see Darren took the coward's way out. He did not want God's love ..." Jack stopped and looked at Kevin. The young, astonished intern, wide-eyed and mouth open, stared at Jack in disbelief. The older jockey averted the gaze, loosened his tied, then continued. "As you can see, this ministry needs your support in reaching out to people like Darren, so that no one will find out the hard way that you can't live without God. If you would like to make a tax-deductible donation ..."

DANGEROUS TONIGHT

Brandon stared at his mother. Somewhere between stoned and coherent, she mumbled. It was not discernable. She struggled to keep her eyes open, as if huge weights tried to bring them down. Barely open, it was unlikely she saw anything, except for her dry, matted hair that draped her eyes. The hair was somewhere between brown and blonde, just like Brandon's.

Pain flared in his jaw. It was because of Harris. Brandon sucked his cheeks together, almost biting them in frustration, anger, and hate. His jaw vibrated, sending sirens of pain through his head. He did not know why he bothered trying to tell her. The last time he told her about Harris punching him, she shook her head. "He brings home the money. It's his house. He makes the rules."

Angry, he listened to his stomach. It growled, folding on itself. The empty pangs rang nervously, frighteningly, and desperately. "Is there anything to eat?"

"I ain't your goddamn cook," she said, almost awakening from her stupor. "You get it yourself."

Brandon turned hard, pounding his feet with every step. Everything seemed to sync: his pounding stomps, the painful throbs resonating from his jaw, and the panging in his stomach. They worked together and fueled his anger. He avoided his stepdad's eyes trudging past him. For three years, it was not only the punches, the snide remarks, but also the disparaging glare from his stepdad, Harris. The old man's eyes often cast an angry glare, then he sighed and shook his head disdainfully.

A shadow bumped into him. "It's the worm-boy," the shadow whispered. Brandon, having enough, finally let the anger shoot through his fist and belted his stepbrother. Immediately, Greg retaliated. First a hit to the nose. Then, the larger boy wrapped his elbow around Brandon's neck. Brandon, unable to breathe, panicked. Three quick punches landed on his stomach and then Greg's knee kicked him in the balls.

"Way to go, Greggy! Kick his ass!" yelled Emily

Brandon hit the floor, guarding his mid-section with his arms, and clutching his testicles with his hands. He took short breaths, trying to get any air back into his lungs. It seemed he needed air even more while in such pain. Emily made a point to kick him in the back, although there was not much to it. He wanted to grab her foot, yank it hard to the left and wrench it broken. Discretion, though won. If he retaliated, her dad, Harris, would certainly take it out on him even worse.

Rolling on his side, he saw Max. The vicious Rottweiler growled as its ears folded back. The dog snarled then let loose a series of barks and finished with a biting snap. "Get away from me you goddam mutt." The dog charged at Brandon, barked and snapped at his arm.

Brandon could not discern whom he hated more. Harris, Greg, Emily, his mother – or that vicious sociopathic dog. Max had bitten him a few times. Of course, it was always his fault, at least according to Harris. Ironically two bites happened when he tried to give Max a treat, like a potato chip or a dog treat. He thought it might get him on Max's good side. He discovered the dog, like its masters, did not have a good side.

"Come on, Max," said Greg while pulling the dog by his collar. "He ain't worth it."

Finding some replenished air in his lungs, and feeling the pain in his groin dissipate, he slowly got up and went to his only place of escape: his room. He sat on the edge of his bed. Letting his eyes adjust to the dark, he captured sight of his laptop. For a second, he wanted to play some games. No. Maybe that book his English Teacher let him check out would help him forget. No. A few episodes of the Walking Dead on Netflix? No. Nothing could help him forget the pain. The hate, like a dying candle flame, found new energy. His anger was the oxygen that fed it. He had to get out of the house.

Within a minute, Brandon's feet pounded the pavement. He glanced back at the house for a split second. As usual, he had no idea where to go. His aimless trek mirrored his life. It was a serialized wandering from one place to the other. Perils, pratfalls, and pressure loomed at every turn, every fork, and every decision. However, there were no possibilities or potential at any of those junctions. Between the drinking, the drugs, the sibling rivalries, and the parent situations, it seemed hopeless. He felt as if he could not breathe in that house – partly because of the smell. Mom hardly ever cleaned anything, and her idea of cooking for the family was sticking some instant Macaroni and Cheese in the microwave.

After a few abrupt, angry turns, he found his anger dissipating. It was almost as if his home that stoked the anger and despair faded as he moved further away. It lost power over him and he found his own gait, his own self, and his own purpose. He still had no idea what that purpose was, but for now, getting away from the house was one that was good enough.

He noticed his visible breath, falling apart and fading into nothing. It did not matter if his huffs exited his mouth or nose, his life force dissipated and disappeared. The recent rains and cold air also tried to chill his skin. Despair overwhelmed his soul. It felt lost. Somehow, he found a fiery anger burning. Pulling his coat tighter, and shoving his hands deeper into the pockets, he hunched his shoulders. He thought of sleeping outside in the dark cold. It seemed fitting to his life. What he had back there was no home.

A lonely light beckoned him. He heard distant

music that called him, piquing his curiosity. Nearly 11 p.m., it was the only sign of life on the small pothole ridden street. Cars parked in the street and driveways were older models, many with damage of either time or other vehicles. The houses, too, were decrepit, often having burnt out porch lights, as well as slanted, uneven porches, tattered windowsills, and discolored siding.

The house ahead called him. Not just with the music and light, but also with curiosity, and a desire for companionship. He just wanted someone to listen to his frustrations of lost hope and his search for something else. Maybe they could help him find some sort of path out of this place full of dead ends and meandering paths.

The door was partially ajar, holding back a subtle, hazy red light. Strange shadows scurried across walls and the ceiling, indicating movement. One shadow jumped up and stretched across the back wall. Brandon stepped back, feeling a dreadful cold within the house. A subtle apprehension lifted within his stomach. It felt like tiny bugs crawled inside, moving up into his chest, growing in number. Soon, his lower jaw quivered. Taking a huge breath, he pushed the door back and stepped in.

Something moved from behind the door. A faint shadow wisped by the corner of his eye. Almost jumping, he thought of leaving. Taking another step, he looked for anyone or anything. Nothing. The red light was actually three lava lamps, all using dark light in the red spectrum. It cast strange shadows as it rolled down the walls, and across the floor and ceiling.

The distorted bass music came from below. A dark stairwell descended, with part of the red-light dancing, spiraling towards the bottom. Part of him wanted to run as the tiny bugs within creeped up to his neck, and spread down his arms, hands, and even fingers. A strange anticipation seemed to take hold of his stomach and pulled. It was an ominous curiosity that wanted to find the forbidden, dangerous mystery. The oak wood step moaned like a man in pain. The next one creaked longer. Unable to see the steps, he took a hold of the handrail to act as a guide. His eyes focused on the door at the base of the stairs. Slightly cracked, he saw a stronger, more prevalent light. It seemed friendlier than the menacing dark red that surrounded him. Reaching the bottom of the steps, he took a breath to calm his shaking limbs. "Hello?"

The music stopped. A bunch of whispers emanated. It sounded like the scattering of mice or rats. Shadows dashed everywhere. Again, an urge to run shot through his legs. Following that, a paralyzing cold seized them. "Hello? Sorry, but the door was open. Is everything okay?" After he stammered words, he pushed the door open. It creaked, swinging back and letting in more light.

Brandon froze, seeing the gun pointed at him. The other boy, about his age, naked from the waist up, lowered the gun. "Brandon? Is that you?" The boy lowered the firearm.

Brandon's chest relaxed, releasing the horrid fright from his body – although his skin shook as if electricity jumped from every hair. Finally looking at the person, the long, gaunt face had a bit of familiarity. Brandon's mind stretched to link the face with a name. He found the name: Martin. Finding a smile, he rushed forward to shake his hand. "Martin! Where have you been? I haven't seen you at school in over a year."

"I've been going to another school, causing problems there. Giving teachers fits. Picking up girls. Causing hell wherever I go."

Brandon recoiled his hand, feeling the cold in the fingers of his old friend.

"Who's that?"

Brandon glanced at the girl. She had red hair and brown eyes, wearing a black tank-top and jeans. She wore black lipstick, black mascara, and a nose ring. She had a tattoo of a sword on her upper left arm.

"That," said Martin, "is Brandon Marshall. The coolest skateboarder from Vincent Jr. High School. He used to make this jump over the …"

Brandon joined and finished with him, "bench and railing past the trashcan and then roll up on the embankment to the sidewalk every day."

"So why are you walking?"

Finding a smile for the first time in a long time, he shook his head. "My stepdad took it away for punching my stepbrother."

"Is he still the asshole you told me about?"

"He's even worse." The smile faded. "I just wish I could just once punch him in the nose and break it then plummet his head into the floor." His words sharpened and dulled at the same time, using them as bludgeons and knives into the people he grew to hate. "And my stepsister, I would carve her tongue out and dangle it front of her, then bite her nose off. My stepbrother, if I could, I'd bash his head into the wall until his swelled shut. And my worthless mom should be cut open and have her guts spilled out!"

Martin's left mouth lifted as he turned towards the red light. The shade from his bangs cast a mischievous, almost sinister glare. Behind the shade, one of the eyes seemed to glow with a red tint. His head dropped. He took a step forward. "Sounds like you had the same problem I had a year ago. An incessant, whining mother, her lousy boyfriend who would get drunk, throw empty beer cans at me, and his scum-sucking son who … well let's just say he didn't give me a choice on my first sexual experience."

Martin moved slowly, and his words got cold, numbing Brandon's skin. Shadows entrapped him, swirling around, dancing among the reddish, bizarre lights. He could not tell if they were people, or objects. Whatever they were, he felt a definite, cold, malevolent presence. Edging closer, Brandon's heart pumped hard where he could almost hear the beat and fill his veins with the hot blood.

"I showed 'em," said Martin. "They will never hurt me again, bother me again, or mistreat me again. They finally found respect for me, not because I placated to them, not because I gained their acceptance, but because of something people really crave: power." Brandon started to feel sleepy. Unable to look away or turn his ears, his eyes focused solely on Martin. Nothing else registered: the lights, the loud music, nor any other thing. "And here's the thing, Brandon, I can give some to you. Use it well, use it wisely, and you'll get much more than you'll ever imagine. There are a few drawbacks, sure, but trust me, the benefits exceed the cost."

Almost hypnotized, Brandon's heart felt at ease. Relaxed, every muscle felt loose. In fact, he had to flex his legs to stay erect. With heavy eyelids, he somehow nodded, finding the offer tempting. What were the costs? He could not understand. The voice got muffled, almost like growling whispers. What were the benefits? Unsure, they must be immeasurable. His body changed from cold to warm. The shadows that circled him and got closer, somehow weaving his eyes shut.

A scream! Another. A yell. A maniacal laugh. Another scream. A shooting pain pulsated through his thigh, into his legs, chest, arms, and head. At first the pain tied knots in the muscles and fired a searing heat in his vessels. It was followed by a numbing cold that crawled like snakes through the inside of his chest and stomach. It did not tickle. It hurt like pin pricks. Curling up like a ball, he fell to the floor, guarding his trunk. It did not help as the pain continued to fire through his body.

His eyes opened. Exhausted, he took a long, deep breath. The air needed to find its way deep, to replenish him. Finding some strength in his limbs, he pulled himself to sit up. His joints fired. His shoulders, his elbows, his stomach muscles, knees and ankles hurt incessantly. Every tiny move triggered an explosion of dull, achy pain that reverberated in his body.

Still in the basement, he looked around. A couple of girls lay on a dingy ecru couch. One had red, curly hair pulled away from her forehead. She was the one he saw last night. She wore a tight, revealing blouse that acted like a magnet for his eyes. Her breasts seemed to summon him. The other had dark hair that draped the corner of her left eye. Both girls had the same dark eyes. Not brown, nor a dark blue, but rather black – shaped like some sort of predator animal. Also, their eyes possessed no emotion but emitted a thick arrogance that bordered on lust. Brandon noticed their pale, ashen skin – making them look anemic.

The dark-haired girl wore a tank-top, showing off some tattoos on her arms, including an upside-down cross. Another was something demonic with intricate drawings. Leaning over, she let her breasts hang low in the tank top, triggering Brandon's young, primal lust.

"I'm Zadie," said the dark-haired girl.

"Hi. I'm Anna," said the red-haired girl.

Realizing he was naked, humiliation and panic seized his mind. Not seeing his clothes, Brandon covered himself with his hands.

The girls both snickered at him. "He wasn't so shy last night," said Anna, "was he?" The girls both giggled.

Brandon, embarrassed, found his clothes on a ratty old recliner that looked as if it had been clawed and ripped as stuffing fell out. Cats? Dogs? No. None were around. He used the back of the chair to hide himself as he struggled to put on his clothes. It was hard as his joints flared with pain. Moreover, his head throbbed as if keeping time with his heartbeat. It tried to steal his coherence and equilibrium. His vision, still hazy at the corners, deteriorated in the distance. It felt as if he still lingered in a dream, or perhaps a trance. He wondered if he had sex with the girls. *Great*, he thought, *I finally get laid, and I can't remember it.*

A third girl, Melissa, emerged from behind a door in the back corner. She also had dark hair and had the same eyes as Anna and Zadie. She only wore jeans and came out topless. Brandon's eyes widened not just at their beauty, but also her cavalier attitude towards strutting around topless.

"There he is." Martin strutted down the stairs. He only wore jeans, showing off his lean torso and muscles. His abs stretched into six neat rows. His chest, squared and firm, would be the envy of any 14-

year-old boy, yet his skin was pale. Pushing up the long, dark bangs revealed both eyes for a second, but they dropped as if trying to hide his identity. "Enjoy your sleep, buddy?"

"I guess so," said Brandon as he put on his boxers and jeans. He then straightened his unkempt sand-brown hair. "What happened? How'd I get ..." After a few stammers, he whispered to Martin, "did I get laid?

"You started acting weird," he said almost laughingly, "then you took off your clothes and started running around in front of Anna, Zadie and Melissa. We got a good laugh."

Embarrassed, Brandon's head fell back, his eyes pressed shut and his hands hid his face. "Shit," he whispered several times to himself. He noticed the girls failing to stifle their subtle laughs. However, the humiliation faded as a throbbing pain pounded within his head. It tried to push through his eyes. "What?" he asked as the pulsing resounded like a drum. "What'd you give me? Pot? Something else?"

Martin held something wrapped in a blanket underneath his arm. Something wriggled while emitting a high-pitched, muffled scream. Martin smiled and tossed the blanket on the floor. The girls converged like ravenous wolves, tearing the thing in the blanket apart. It screamed so loud, forcing Brandon to cover his ears. He retreated below the recliner's back to hide from the spreading blood, pieces of flesh, hair, and bone across the room. The girls' screams mixed with the child … or was it some sort of animal? His heart thudded viciously, almost hurting and spreading a fiery feeling down his chest, arms, hips, and legs. Following the raging heat was a tingling cold that seized the hairs on his skin.

It was quiet. Brandon stood, trying to focus his eyes. He tried to discern as to what was wrapped in the blanket. A dog? A cat? A possum? No. It had four appendages, but they looked like … Brandon shook his head, unsure if he saw an arm with a human hand. Could it have been a baby? Or perhaps a toddler no more than two or three? No … they wouldn't have ripped apart and eaten a child? Or would they?

The girls gathered in the middle of the room. They all tilted her heads back, slurping the blood, licking their lips, and smacking on the flesh. An immense amount of blood dripped down their jaws, their chins, and their breasts. Color suddenly rushed to their skin as they inhaled deeply while stretching. Martin walked over to them and kissed them one at a time. He kissed them on the neck, letting his lips press tightly, licking off the blood for himself, gulping it hard, letting a lot of it cascade down his naked chest. The girls licked the syrupy blood off his chest and abs. His neck arched back as his breaths came in deep huffs. He relaxed as the shadows gathered around him. He laughed subtly as his eyes reddened in the abysmal dark.

Brandon, unsure of what he saw, had to get out of there and report that they killed a small baby or a child.

And they ate him or her! What was going on? Some sort of Satanic Cannibalistic ritual? Occult worship? Or did he imagine the whole thing? Did he dream it?

Walking past Martin, wanting to leave as quickly as he could, his footsteps echoed in the dark, enclosed hallway. Reaching the top of the stairs, he glanced back at the dancing red light that swirled into a continuous eddy. It seemed like an entrance into another dimension. Looking ahead, he jumped, almost falling backwards down the stairs. The girls, somehow cleaned of the blood, stood in front of him. How did they get up here? How did they get their skin perfectly cleansed of the blood? They stared at him, full of beauty and a sexual allure.

They whispered.

"Be one of us."

"Come back later tonight."

"Stay with us."

"Help us."

The whispers kept echoing. He had to leave before they confused him. Although he felt cold, his heart raced and sweat poured from his skin. Shaking, unable to control it, he rushed outside and faced the cracks of light barely emerging in the east. It was like waking up and turning on the light as his eyes cringed and hurt. The door behind him slammed.

The fear dissipated as his muscles relaxed. The electricity in his nerves dissipated, and his heart relaxed. More importantly, his eyes stopped hurting as they adjusted to the light of day. Should he go home and stay there for the day? No. However, he didn't have too much time to go back, get his backpack and get to school.

***

Brandon walked in a fog all day. The fog was not vapors fueled by the sun, but one inside his mind as he struggled to maintain balance and focus on basic tasks. Even though he didn't fall asleep, he couldn't remember if he rode the bus or walked to school. He didn't remember first period at all. In a way, it felt as if he was the only one there. Did he have an assignment? Did he do it? Second period, English, was the same. In fact, did he eat breakfast? Did he have lunch? Hunger pains in his gut craved something, but not candy or chips from the vending machines, or even pop. What did those assholes do to him?

The light beat heavily on Brandon's eyes as he walked into fourth period biology. Almost hurting, his eyelids clamped tight, and he shook his head. His headache pounded so much, he made a point to avert the classroom window where the sun filtered through some high cirrus clouds. Reaching into his backpack, he pulled out his sunglasses and tried to put them on.

A hand quickly removed the sunglasses from his face. "I don't think so, Mr. Marshall." Mr. Darnell, the science teacher, put the glasses on his podium. "You can get them after class."

As soon as the bell rang, Brandon seized them on

the way out and put them on. They did help some, but the sunlight breaking through the windows still overwhelmed him. Shutting his eyes, turning his head, the vibration in his mind pulsed loudly. It seemed angry. A mishmash of voices confused him. He could only decipher small bits.

"He's so scummy."

"Lose control."

"Watch it, dickwad."

"Join us."

"It'll be alright."

"Play in the dark forever."

"What's wrong will soon be right."

The noise stopped rendering the hallways of students silent. He saw his stepsister, Emily, as she huddled in a corner with her friends. Her mouth had a ring in the lower lip, and one on the upper lip on the opposite side. Another ring went through her left nostril. He saw his stepsister pull out a razor blade and cut the area between two knuckles.

The sound of blood bursting through her skin sounded like distant thunder. He inhaled deeply through his nose to savor the salty, tempting scent her blood gave. Brandon licked his lips. Somehow, he heard Emily's heart pump. He had an urge to draw more blood. Stomach pains goaded him to rip out her heart and eat it.

The bell pulled him from the stupor and students scattered like cockroaches revealed after turning on a light. He rushed to the locker room, wondering what was wrong with him. Maybe he should go to the nurse's office. No. He'll be alright.

Getting to the dim locker room, his eyes felt better. He struggled with getting his gym shorts and shirt on as the pain in his joints continued their throbbing pain. It even hurt to bend at the waist. "Oh, fuckin' shit," he said quietly. "What those assholes do to me?" He kept thinking about talking to a teacher, or perhaps a counselor of the early, pre-dawn murder he saw. Or was it murder? Was it an animal? Unsure, it seemed like trying to grasp the fog or perhaps capture water in his hands. Brandon could not wait to get home and sleep.

"What is up with you?"

He turned to his friend, Billy, and shook his head. "I don't know. I went to this small … party last night and I … woke up feeling shitty."

"Didja get drunk or high?"

Again, shaking his head, Brandon tried to remember. "I don't know." The secret begged to come out. He had to get it off his chest. "I think they murdered a little kid or a baby early this morning."

"What?"

"There was screaming, blood everywhere. They ate it like a bunch of … hungry dogs. Jesus, they ripped off an arm." It was the only clear memory, bringing back the terror of the sight and sounds. He wanted to cry, but it turned into a sinister laugh. Why?

Did he find it funny? Or was it some sort of defense mechanism?

"Are you sure it wasn't a cat or a dog? And why are you laughing about it?"

By now, they were in full gym clothes and were walking towards the basketball courts. Brandon shook his head. "I don't know. I just …" He failed to grasp the full memory, despite its hideous nature, and the terror at that one moment. What was it they killed?

Brandon and Billy were on the skins team. The basketball dribbling irritated his head, but somehow, he found some energy. Amazingly, his senses heightened. He passed the ball with ease and caught with just the same agility. He seemed to have incredible speed. What was going on? At this point, he liked it. As his heartbeat increased, the blood flowed and warmed him greatly. His muscles came alive. His eyes now focused on the basket. One shot went right in without any effort. Within a few minutes, he was huffing but did not feel tired. He got another pass and jumped to take a shot. He slammed the ball into a hoop.

After dropping to the floor, he saw the basketball bounce once, then flattened on the floor. Stunned by the silence, tilted his head and brushed the long hair out of his eyes. One boy picked up the deflated ball and inspected it. The others gathered around, as well as Coach Doyle. Brandon remained at a distance and noticed: slits in the ball. About a finger-length apart, it looked as if a knife or razor blade has sliced through.

He kept looking at his nails, then at the flat, airless basketball.

Brandon glanced at his hands. His fingernails had not just grown but also sharpened and honed as if to inflict damage. Hiding his hands, he touched his inner left thigh, feeling a couple sets of bumps. Glancing down, he saw them: puncture wounds as if something bit him there.

Remembering how he slam-dunked the basketball, he glanced at the basket. It was ten feet off the floor – and he was only five foot, four inches tall. He jumped ten feet, high enough to slam-dunk the ball?

Confused, almost scared, he turned around and returned to the locker room. Wanting to look normal and not attract attention, he kept his gait focused, yet quick. His steps almost synced with his heartbeat. Reaching the locker, he took a deep breath and closed his eyes. His fingers pressed tightly onto the locker grills. Hearing the metal on the locker crunch, he noticed his fingers easily twisted the locker door out of shape.

What was happening? Martin and those girls definitely did something to him. What, though? Inject him with some sort of drug? It was after he was hypnotized. Maybe when he was asleep. He could not remember … wait. It came back.

He screamed as Anna backed away from him. Before she unlocked their lips, she bit his lower lip hard. He pulled off his shirt while screaming – actually howling. Zadie lifted her head from his crotch area. She hissed at him like a cat and let a drop of blood hit his thigh. Her eyes widened. It seemed her incisors had lengthened. He felt the pain in his inner thigh. Her teeth grew as her cheeks lifted high – as if getting ready to bite him. She bit his nipple – causing a rippling pain as well as some strange euphoric sensation.

A hand fell on his shoulder, pulling him from the forgotten memory. "Okay, Marshall, what the hell just happened?"

Brandon shook his head, refusing to turn around and face Coach Doyle. The guy was massive, with huge shoulders, and an expansive chest. Moreover, he stood over six feet tall. The gym coach did play linebacker for some pro football team for two years, so he was very intimidating.

"Marshall? Are you on something?" The frustrated coach pulled on Brandon's shoulder again. "Turn around and face me!"

As Brandon was spun around, his hand clasped down on Coach Doyle's wrist. He squeezed tightly. Somehow, his fingernails lengthened, driving themselves into the coach's skin. Brandon enjoyed watching the grown man fall to his knees – even more so as he yelled. Hissing, Brandon yanked the man's arm, relishing the sound of snapping bones.

A feeling somewhere between pain and pleasure erupted in his gums. His incisors grew and sharpened. His head stretched as his mouth grew and his ears lengthened. Hearing the coach's heartbeat and rushing blood, a painful hunger erupted into a simmering anger, then festered to a vile hatred.

Grabbing the adult by his neck, Brandon stared into his eyes. A petrified look washed across the man's face. He desperately tried to get a breath.

"Don't ever touch me again." Brandon's voice sounded somewhere between human and animal, whisper and yell, and between fear and anger. He shoved the coach and let go. Coach Doyle flew about five or six feet backwards, slamming him into the lockers.

Brandon dressed in his street clothes and left school.

***

His jaw dropped again. Looking at the public library computer, Brandon saw the headline: "Three-year-old boy missing." Brandon read about it:

"Police are still searching for three-year-old Devon Wilde who disappeared last night shortly after 8 p.m. The boy was outside with his mother, Ellen Wilde, and his sister, Alice. The two went inside the house to get some more Halloween decorations for the lawn, and when they returned found him gone. After searching for him in three neighbors' houses, they called the

police. So far ..."

Brandon's breath froze. Martin and his girls surely murdered the child. Why would they kill a defenseless child? A three-year-old? The shock lifted in his soul, only to be dragged away with a biting anger. For some reason, he grinned at the thought of tearing a person apart and mangling their corpse.

He slammed his fist on the library computer desk. It left a crack and garnered some of the patrons' attention. *What the fuck is wrong with me? I reveled in a little kid's death? Why didn't I stop them. I sat there and did NOTHING.*

Clenching his eyes tight, he tried to release some tears. Regret, sadness washed through quickly but faded into nothing. Somehow, for some bizarre reason, he could not find any tears, but rather ... laughter and delight.

Shaking aside the gamut of emotions, he did a few other search engines. The first was "Missing Children Anna." He saw her picture – and it was definitely her. Anna Dreydon, from Freeport, PA was reported as missing a year ago. Police suspected foul play because they found her blouse that had blood on it. He tried a search on Melissa. Yes – that was definitely her! She was reported missing from Weister, PA in ... 1991? That was 34 years ago! How could she still look as if she's 14 or 15? Zadie, actually a runaway, was reported missing from Akron, OH in 2010.

He started to pull out his smart phone to call the police. He dialed 9, then 1, but stopped. Wait? What if they were after him? He had assaulted Coach Doyle. What if they did a drug test and found drugs in him? He could go to juvenile prison. Would they believe him about three missing kids, and a fourth one murdered? His mom and stepdad would not believe him. Would he be considered responsible for the murder as well? What if those kids shoved the blame on him?

A text alert vibrated. He glanced at it. "Get your stupid ass home now!" It was from Harris. Emily probably told him what happened. Or maybe Greg did. One time Greg and Emily told Harris that Brandon was shooting up with heroin. It wasn't true. Brandon was scared of needles. It didn't matter to Harris. He just punched Brandon in the nose, almost breaking it. Anger simmered as he recalled lying to the Emergency Room doctor that he was punched by a kid he knew from school. If he hadn't, Harris would have made it worse. Mom used the old stand-by excuse: "He gives us a home."

Brandon left the library.

***

His hand hurt. Brandon didn't care, pounding the door again several times. A couple of deep cracks had formed on the door. Even though he wore sunglasses, he flinched seeing the sun retreat beneath the horizon. About the only thing left was an orange hue that scattered light on the underside of the clouds. A wind blew. A sharp chill bit his skin. Strangely, he acclimated almost immediately. Usually, he had low tolerance for cold. It seemed appropriate now. More appropriately, the long shadows of trees and homes stretched into oblivion as light retreated from this side of the world – letting the darkness creeped in.

Brandon pounded on the door again. The crack he made deepened. Knocked loose from the deadbolt, the door swung ajar. Barely visible, silhouetted behind an interior light, he caught a glimpse of a girl's figure. Amidst the dark shadow, a subtle red glow emanated from where eyes would be. Something horrible smelled. It spread out as she spoke. "Hey, cutie," it sounded like Anna. "Glad to see you came back."

"I need to talk to Martin."

Zadie appeared. "Hey there," she winked, "… nice to see you again."

"What the hell did you do to me? Where's Martin?"

Martin emerged from shadow, appearing in the glow of the ominous red circling light. His arm was around Melissa. "Let him in." Did their eyes have a subtle red glow, too?

"What the hell did you do to me?" ask Brandon. "What's going on? How can I … jump high? Beat up my coach? You mentioned your parents don't bother you. How? Why? Where are they? Why did you kill that little boy?"

"Why do you think? I'm surprised you haven't figured it out by now."

"What did you do to me?" he yelled, storming into the house. "What are you?"

Martin's eyes, visible, shortened and widened. An ominous, red glow radiated as he hissed, opened his mouth and displayed his fangs. The face changed. Elongated ears, dry, gray skin, hideous scars, and a longer, pointed nose.

Terrified, Brandon felt a chill. It started within, working its way out. The deathly cold spread from his heart, which seemed to be lulled to a slower beat. It reached his skin, forcing him to retreat from Martin. His mind calmed as all emotions vacated his soul.

Martin sneered. "You want in, don't you? Admit it. You want companionship, company, and autonomy. Free from parents, their rules, their disdain and hatred for you. Free from responsibility and constraints. Teachers who don't care, siblings who are ambivalent. We can give what you crave for: acceptance and attention. You watch our backs, we watch yours. We sleep together, play together, work together, and eat together. Was that a home you came from? There certainly was no home for me. Or them. Join us."

The girls now surrounded him. They had changed. Their skin paled white, then turned to a cadaver like blue. Their ears sharpened. Their hair grew, along with their fingernails. Fangs spread from their mandible. Eyes became cat-like, having a subtle, yellow glow.

"I can't eat kids," he stammered. "I can't kill people."

"Give me a break!" The exploding voice startled him. "This isn't fucking Twilight. That's fantasy, fairy tale shit. We're bad guys. Evil. We trap. We kill. We eat. We draw blood." Martin's voice calmed, almost becoming hypnotic. A deep bass chuckle emanated from his throat. It lulled Brandon into a trance. "Besides, usually we get some homeless bum no one cares about. Or we swipe a freshly aborted fetus that is still slightly alive. Hell, the clinic does the dirty work and all we do is sneak in for a meal. They're nameless – just like you were. Like we were. No one cared about us. Until we met each other. You're hungry as hell – aren't you?"

Brandon felt the hunger that hollowed him out. Martin going on about it made his stomach emptier, more painful, and lonelier.

"It's really great," said Zadie. "We take what we want. A stolen purse, smart phone, or wallet, and we have what we need. No state services to bug us. No schools to deal with. Visit a basketball or football game, and we can find some new ones to tempt. Another nameless person to gorge on, draw blood and life from."

Anna moved closer to him, returning to human form. She whispered in his ear while "Join us. We can have a lot of fun. No rules, just us." Although her breath stank, the whispers lured him into sleepiness. The touch on his hair, his skin, and shoulders made him feel alive. It stimulated him sexually. Liking it, he listened intently. "If not, we can just feed off your blood right now. Instead, we're giving you a real offer. Be with us."

Melissa stood opposite Anna, and she, too, whispered in his ear. She kissed his neck gently. Her fingernails raked the nape of his neck. It felt wonderful. She rubbed his chest. "Help us find new food, money, new lives, and some new recruits. Stain your soul to red from white."

Brandon felt it. His skin crackled. It felt cold. It dried. His ears sharpened, as well as his fangs that almost grew by merely thinking about it. He rushed to the mirror to see it. He felt it for years, but now he finally saw his image fade into oblivion. He knew that was what Mom, Harris, Greg and Emily saw: nothing. His true essence now borne to his eyes. A lost soul with no home. He found what he was looking for. No longer would he be a punching bag for his lousy excuse of a family. He'll be dangerous tonight.

***

Brandon, low, approached his house. He turned himself into a wolflike dog – which was a bit painful. However, his mind remained, as well as his heightened senses of sight, smell, and sound. Looking up, he saw the police car casting its alternating lights of red, blue, and yellow. They flashed slowly, not enough to confuse anyone, but enough to disturb the tranquil night. He moved closer towards the bush as the police knocked on his front door. He watched them.

The door opened. Harris, as usual, had a beer in his hand. His flabby, yet somewhat muscular physique peeked through his shirt – along with the stray chest and back hairs. His curly, unkempt sandy-brown hair looked as if it had not been cleaned in days. Stubble was scattered across his jaw, emerging into a fluffy goatee beard. "What's this?" he asked.

"Sir," said one officer, "is this the residence of Brandon Marshall?"

"What the hell did he do, now?"

"We need to place him under arrest. He assaulted his gym teacher today at school."

Harris looked back into the house. "Is that little shit home, yet? Where's Brandon?"

Emily came to the door, along with Brandon's mother. Both asked what was going on and got the same story.

"Sir, can you please let us in to see if he is here."

"You got a warrant?"

The second officer handed him a document, so Harris stepped aside. Finally, the asshole did the smart thing when dealing with a cop. Brandon turned from the bush and rushed around the side of the house. He heard them inside. His mom kept yelling at them as the police looked behind every room and closet door. "He is not here. And what are you going to do to him?"

"Ma'am, we have a warrant for his arrest."

Brandon, still in the form of an alpha canine, looked up to see Greg who dropped to a knee and extended his hand to pet him. "Hey boy, what are you doing here?"

Brandon snapped at the hand that tried to pet him. Greg backed away and tried to kick him. Brandon snarled, then bit Greg's ankle hard, clamping hard and wrestling his foot away. Greg continued to cuss, trying to pull his leg away. "Goddamn mutt. I'm gonna shoot you with my gun." Brandon growled hard, snapping, snarling, chasing Greg back inside the house.

As the wolf hound, Brandon stared into Greg's eyes. His stepbrother lost all comprehension. His eyes narrowed, his smile faded, and no emotion emanated from his eyes. Lulled listless, he stood and quietly opened the back screen door. Greg's handgun dropped to the floor.

Brandon strode in through the kitchen. Max looked at him. Brandon's wolf glare commanded Max to run away. For the first time ever, Max yelped as he ran away from Brandon, or rather the wolf hound. Stopping in the shadows next to the staircase, Brandon watched the police starting to leave. "Sir, please give us a call if he returns home. We will continue to look for him."

"If you find him," said Harris, "just shoot him."

"Please don't hurt my baby, officer," said Mom, "please."

The police light bar ceased its dance, rendering the night dark. Brandon backed into the shadows, hiding in the darkness. Mom drew the curtains. His canine, nocturnal eyes adjusted quickly. His ever-sensitive ears picked up griping, cussing, and frustrated whispers. He even heard Emily. The smells reached his nostrils: beer, cigarettes, dirty laundry, dog hair, and a damp, moldy aroma. Brandon glanced back at Greg, who still stared ahead at nothing, while standing in the dark kitchen. The screen door let the chill of the evening air seep in, stealing the warmth of the wooden floor.

Footsteps thundered down the stairs, startling him. It was time. Brandon stealthily moved near the basement door, trapped in the darkest shadows. He only had to think, command at will, and it happened. The fur retreated. His eyes rounded as the snout receded into his face, and the black, wet nose retreated into human form. From his rear paws, toes emerged, and his legs lengthened. Fingers emerged from his front paws. Both front legs became bare, then morphed into a human skeletal structure. It hurt. He kept his groans a whisper as he returned to human form. He stood, naked in the shadows, waiting for the right moment.

Harris reached the bottom of the stairs. His head tilted as if alerted to a tiny sound. "Greg?" He moved into the kitchen and whispered. "Son? What are you …?" His voice trailed as if confused.

Brandon cast his hateful glare at Harris, remaining

silent, patient and letting the hate surge. He noticed the mirror that only showed Harris moving towards the kitchen with no hint of Brandon behind him.

"My, God, what's that fucking smell?"

Brandon laughed in a whisper, letting his true form appear in the mirror for a split second. He relished the terror in Harris eyes, and how his skin paled as the color retreated. However, the look faded as Brandon made himself disappear.

Harris sighed, then turned face-to-face with Brandon. His eyes widened and his muscles flexed as Brandon screeched at him. The sound forced Harris to cover his ears and retreat to the wall. Brandon shoved his claws deep into Harris' abdomen. Blood splattered across the already stained walls, then slowly rolled down towards the floor. Harris' rotund stomach, sliced apart, and spilled fat, innards, and blood to the floor. At the same time, Brandon inserted thick fangs into his stepdad's neck, tearing the jugular and tasting the warm, delicious blood that ran down his tongue, throat and stomach. One bite, and he savored the warm, fresh blood. Remembering this was Harris' blood, Brandon spit it out.

Brandon enjoyed the carnage until a chair crashed on his back and split apart. Brandon faced Greg who tried to stab Brandon with a kitchen knife. Brandon caught his stepbrother's wrist. Twisting back, he heard the bone snap. Greg screamed a barrage of profanity while falling to his knees. "Max, sic'em."

Max growled subtly and angrily. The dog lowered his ears and head, ready to pounce. Brandon stared at the vicious canine and easily found the command. Max turned and pounced at Greg, knocking him to the ground. Max, in a frenzy, scratched, snarled, and bit at Greg until he snapped the jugular. Blood stained the already dingy floor.

Brandon heard the two sets of footsteps race down the stairs and towards the kitchen. He jumped high, flipped, and sank his foot claws into the ceiling to stay hidden for a brief moment. The light switch clicked. The bulbs brightened the room. Mom and Emily screamed at the sight. "Max, no!" The dog let loose of Greg who continued writhing for a few seconds until he slumped. His last breath gurgled as his chest flattened.

Brandon sliced the ceiling lights with his claw, sending glass debris everywhere. Mom ducked, Emily cried. He dropped before them, revealing his fangs and demonic face. Both women retreated to the living room. Again, he found the right voice, the one thought for command – and Max chased his mother. The dog growled as it kept snapping at her relentlessly. Her arms tried to keep him away to no avail. Its jaws scattered both flesh and blood.

One leap, and Brandon snatched Emily, flipped upside down and shoved his foot claws into the ceiling. Holding onto her, Emily kicked and screamed, begging Brandon to spare her. His howling laughter made her shriek. Panic set in, and she desperately tried to writhe herself free from his strong grip. Curbing his hisses and howls, he quietly glared into her eyes and discovered the right stare

Transfixed, her breaths slowed, and all personality left her eyes – leaving behind a blank expression. Somehow, she whispered his name. "Brandon, please. I'm so sorry."

He stared at her for a moment, noticing her beauty. Yet, he found her disgusting and repugnant. Harris was her dad, so that would make anyone unhappy and unfulfilled. Tears emerged from the corner of her eyes, sloping off the inner brows and to the floor. Brandon heard the tear splash on the floor. Gazing into her eyes again, he sighed.

"Please, please," she said. "I'm so sorry." Her voice faded to silence and Brandon heard the thumping of her heart.

She tried to cover her ears as he howled. With one snap, one bite, he tore her neck away. While she gurgled her last breath, he let go, dropping her to the floor. He followed, swinging his legs to land on his feet. His quiet, psychic command allowed Max to let go of Mom. She cried, grunted, and rolled over. Her eyes, beyond shock, beyond terror, looked at her bloodied, mangled wounds. Her visible breaths were in short pants. She cried as her lower jaw shook.

Brandon stood before her and squatted to one leg. Warm blood dripped down his lower jaw, underneath his neck, and stained his chest. It started to dry. He felt more blood all over his naked legs. It streamed down over his knees and even got to his feet.

Mom tried to stand. "Baby, please. Try to understand. I'm so sorry." Able to get to her knees, she extended both hands, pleading for her life. "Please. We'll leave this place. We'll find another life. I'll find another man to be your father. Do you want something to eat? I'll make you something."

A deadly quiet ruled the still air. He looked at mom, then at the dark silhouette of Emily, and Harris both slumped on the floor. Was that all she could do? Beg and plea? What about his begging, his pleading over the years? She got quiet as he stared at her. She seemed almost asleep. She wrapped her arms around him and pulled him closer.

Brandon sank his teeth into her neck. He drank heavily. It was good. It was the best meal she ever gave him.

FROM "My Best Friend is a Demon"

Wednesday and Victor

"My name is Elise." I said it again, looking directly at the mirror. "My name is Elise." I tried it one more time. "My name is Elise." That was it! I rid myself of the emotions in saying my name.

I said it a few more times, working on keeping any feeling or empathy from my eyes and voice. Dad and Mom said I reminded them of Wednesday Addams – and after seeing the two movies from the 1990s, I had to perfect my tone and look. The old TV show, while corny, was fun to watch and give me the template for the character as well – although I could not bring myself to wear the stupid looking dress. Also, Wednesday did not have glasses. At first, I wanted a sinister frame to house the lenses, however, I realized my glasses were fine the way they were. They had an innocuous look that added some intellect to my emotionless persona.

Feeling something cold brush across my neck made it snap to the left. Was that cool air flowing from the vent? My hands folded over my chest guarded when a cold finger stroked my right ear. While hairs tingled and shook, my breath locked into place. Looking around, I tried to find whoever did that.

"Elise."

Who was that? I swiveled my chair and stood, trying to locate the whisper.

"Elise."

A steady energy fired through my nerves, creating tremors that seized my fingers, hands, arms, and legs. Strangely, my heart never fell out of sync, nor did my breath run erratically. Within my head, something swirled like a racing house gecko – except he didn't say he'd save me 15 percent on car insurance.

My eyes squinted, noticing the subtle red glow in the closet. I always thought something evil lived in my closet. At night, it looked like a black gateway into pitch darkness. The glow changed to a slight yellow, then back to red. Yellow. Red. Yellow. Red. The colors faded into nothing as I stepped closer to the folding doors that stood slightly ajar.

"Elise."

I'll bet it's Jeffrey teasing me. Our constant goal was to scare each other. It's in our genes, I guess. Mom and Dad also liked to sneak up on us and scare us. Dad used to joke that the morning of the Resurrection of Jesus that he snuck up on the women and said "Boo" which is why people say "Jesus Christ!" when someone sneaks up on them. I never really got that joke, but he and Mom thought it was hilarious. You get that when your parents grew up on horror movies of the 1980s and 1990s.

Now my nose cringed as a dank, disgusting smell reached my nostrils. It stank so bad, I had to turn my head and pinch my eyes shut. It smelled like … like … something. I did not have anything to compare it to.

Something was there on the floor in the closet. I rushed to open the folding doors and reached into attack my brother. The light flooded in – revealing a large teddy bear who had a stupid grin on its face. I kept it to spare Mom and Dad's feelings because I loathe childlike romances and infatuations with the innocence of childhood. I wanted a Chucky Doll, Talky Tina, the Zulu doll from Trilogy of Terror, a Pennywise Doll, and an Anabelle doll from The Conjuring.

The lights flickered. What is going on? As I turned around, it seemed as if the walls closed in. My stomach shifted as the room appeared to tilt to the left. Almost losing my balance, I wondered if the room actually swiveled, or if my perception threw off my steadiness.

My jaw dropped, mimicking the creepy dolls I did have. Their mouths dropped open while their eyelids lifted on their own. I heard the voice again – except it was louder, but no more than a whisper.

"Elise."

"That is so wickedly cool," I muttered. The anxiety in my chest turned to joy. I always wanted a ghost to share a room with. "Holy Mother Mary May I! Are you a ghost?"

"More or less."

I heard the whisper in my ear. "Oh, please let me

be your friend. I've always wanted to be friends with a ghost. What's your name?"

"Victor."

My anticipation deflated, mimicking the sigh I let out. "Oh, great. I get a boy ghost. I already have an annoying brother and a lame cousin. I wanted a ghost sister." Disappointed, I blew out another breath hard – hoping it might be enough to push the ghost away. "Do you have a sister I could be friends with? Please? It's my dream."

"Elise, I will be your friend."

"If I could kick you in the balls – I would."

The lights flickered. All the joy inside me shrank into a ball of ice. Now it emanated a horrid, frightening dread. Uneasy, a deep anxiety spread slowly in my mind. Void of any peace, contentment or hope, I almost cried. Is that what Victor was doing to me? I didn't like it. A bitter cold wrapped around me. A vaporous breath fell from my mouth and nose. Immediately, I clutched my body. Arms tight, I tried to find some warmth. It felt like ice particles formed on my skin, nose, cheeks, and ears.

"Okay, okay," I muttered between chattering my teeth. "I'll be your friend, okay. Okay?"

The frigid air and ominous anxiety faded – although not completely. Taking a deep breath, counted to ten as I closed my eyes, then opened them.

The terror returned in full force as I saw him in the mirror behind me! Although it wore a cloak over its head, the wide slit mouth smiled, spreading over the boundaries of its narrow, sunken cheeks. The eyes, white, rested within a thick blackness. They vibrated, growing into bulbous spreads with red scars. The nose, only two nostrils, also changed in size, pulsating large then shrinking in sync with the eyes. The mouth opened wide, baring teeth that looked chiseled. I felt a hot, dank breath blowing through my hair and spreading over my neck.

The lights flickered then doused, taking the terror in my heart with it. Noticing my erratic breath, I took a few deep breaths, held them, and counted. The image was no longer behind me.

This was so cool.

From the third book in *The Blind Faith Series,*
"My Best Friend is a Demon"

Coming November 2025

ABOUT THE AUTHOR:

Stephen W. Scott was born in Tulsa, OK. He attended the University of Oklahoma and graduated with a degree in Journalism – Professional Writing. He has worked for a few newspapers, then moved to Wilmore, KY in 1991 to attend Asbury Theological Seminary where he received his Master of Divinity in 1995. After returning to Oklahoma, he served as a pastor and chaplain in the United Methodist Conference. He has been working in education since 2001 and resides in Tulsa, OK. He also wrote *"Abandoned,"* along with *"Do You Hear What I Hear?"* and the award-winning book, *"The Demon Inside Me."* He enjoys bicycling, weightlifting, photography, reading, playing guitar and writing.

www.swscott-author.com

<u>Coming in 2026:</u>
"Death Notice"
a prequel to *The Blind Faith Series*

"The Demon and the Vampire"
The fourth book of *The Blind Faith Series*

www.ingramcontent.com/pod-product-compliance
Lightning Source LLC
Chambersburg PA
CBHW071117100726
47908CB00008B/2404